The *Ugly Sweater* PARTY

AURORA ALBA & ODESSA ALBA

The Ugly Sweater PARTY

*If you've ever had a dreamy crush at work
that made your heart flutter...*

This is for you.

Chapter 1

Festive, tree-wrapped string lights refracted on the layer of fresh-fallen snow, glittering like fragments of fine-ground glass. Blistering winter winds whipped across Twila's petite face and rosy cheeks, clawing at the collar of her thick, down jacket.

Winters in lower Manhattan could chill a person straight to the bone, and this year was no exception. Despite the late-December freeze, New Yorkers soldiered through the slush-filled streets seeking last-minute gifts and visiting family. They bustled through the maze of impossibly tall buildings with vigor, eager to escape the clutches of the cold.

Twila sighed with relief when she escaped the blustery, gray afternoon through the building's rotating door.

The warmth of the skyscraper's lobby felt like the embrace of a loving friend, wrapping her tight in its comforting arms. The cloying smell of sugar cookies hung like a dense cloud in the lobby, oozing its sickly sweet aroma from a platter on the front desk.

Like many buildings in Manhattan, the lobby was stunning. The floor was decorated in chevrons of streaked marble, butting cohesively against the inviting, gold texture of the walls. Overhead, a massive chandelier littered with cylindrical crystals glimmered brightly, casting an air of opulence over the cavernous space. In the far corner sat a modest Christmas tree wrapped in amber lights adorned with glittery ornaments. Piped-in holiday classics played quietly throughout the room.

Twila made her way to the front desk, a bulky station of espresso-colored wood. She leaned against its glazed top. "Afternoon, Jessie."

Jessie's caramel-colored face smiled, embarrassed at the mouthful of cookie he'd been gnawing on when she approached. "I'm so sorry," he muttered with a hand over his mouth.

"Don't be!" Twila chuckled. "Did Janice make those?"

He nodded bashfully, still covering the lower half of his face. "Yes, ma'am, she's killing me. She wants me to lose weight and then sends me to work with these things." He dusted his hands off and stood up straight. "They're my kryptonite."

He slid the piled-high plate toward her, and she eyed them momentarily before waving them away. "No, thank you, Jessie. Gotta save myself. One of my coworkers promised to bring in this layered dip that is…" she moaned, "the *best*."

Jessie offered her a pleasant smile. "Fair enough." He beamed, bright and cheery. "By yourself tonight?"

"As usual," she said matter-of-factly, punctuating the comment with a scoff. Her solitude no longer seemed like a choice but a way of life beyond her control.

"I know it's a few days early, but Merry Christmas, Miss Henderson."

"Thank you. Merry Christmas to you and your lovely wife as well. Got anything fun planned with Janice and Stuart?"

She took a few steps past the desk to the wall and pressed the button to call the elevator. She quickly retreated back to the desk to wait for it to arrive.

Jessie shook his head, pleasantly surprised. "Your memory never ceases to astound me. No, Stu is celebrating Christmas at Jan's mother's house this year up in the Catskills. And I think Janice and I are just going to take it easy. Maybe watch a few holiday classics. Drink some eggnog. Nothing major." He leaned forward. "How about you?"

"Oh, Sir Puffington and I will probably gorge on Chinese food and watch Christmas Story reruns while I try not to think about how I let another year pass where I didn't have the guts to take myself ice skating at Rockefeller Center." She chuckled.

"You seem too young and lovely to be a cat-hoarding spinster."

She laughed. "Well, I'm only a level-one spinster. I just have the singular needy feline for now. I imagine every year for my birthday, I will adopt another until I can rival the most intense cat hoarders."

Jessie chuckled and waved a hand at her. "Oh, stop." He typed something on his keyboard and spoke again. "You really should do Rockefeller. It's fun. Jan and I went two years ago. She was like a newborn giraffe, all clumsy. She must have fallen or nearly fallen twenty times. Most adorable thing I've ever seen. We had a great time, though."

"Sounds like me." Twila snickered. "Oh! Do I need to sign in or anything?"

"No, ma'am. Not for the holiday party."

"Okay, great." She adjusted the purple down jacket in her sweater-covered arms and glanced back to the brass doors of the elevator, wishing she could will it to work faster with her mind. She needed some boozy eggnog and some of Mason's seven-layer taco dip in her growling stomach… *stat*.

"Excited for the party?"

"Oh yes. I'm in it to win it this year," she held out her plum-colored coat to show off the hideous Christmas sweater hidden behind it. Garish pine trees with knitted, red garlands lined the neckline. Below, in giant yellow font, the words '*Jingle My Balls*' sat breast-height, made from glued-on felt letters. A pair of pendulous, plastic ornaments hung from the lower hemline, dangling at crotch level like a pair of festive testes.

Jessie shook his head, fighting a grin. "If you *don't*, they're either drunk or crazy."

"Thank you." She curtsied and pulled the maroon beanie from her head, letting loose a mass of long, flaxen waves.

Suddenly, a draft blew in behind her.

Twila knew, even before she looked that only one man in this building was capable of dragging *that* kind of icy energy in with his chilling presence...

Nathan DuPont.

Vice President of *Parramore Medical Supply, Co.*

Stunningly-handsome dickhead.

Nathan rushed in. His raven hair, charcoal parka, and creme-colored cashmere scarf were dusted with snow. His chiseled face was pink from the frigid Manhattan air.

Twila fought the urge to grimace at her employer. Instead, she offered a subtle, respectful nod.

Nathan returned her non-verbal greeting in a cold, obligatory way and brushed briskly through the lobby.

Twila rolled her eyes as he passed. Nathan used to, at the very least, muster a tepid reply. Now it seemed 'Nasty Nate,' office *Grinch*, was always seemingly callous and aloof.

Impatient, Nathan pressed the button several times and rapped his fingers against the leg of his slacks.

"Would you like me to bring you down anything later?" Twila asked the receptionist, voice tinged with sweetness.

"No, thank you, Miss Henderson. You're too kind."

DING!

The elevator sounded. After a moment, it peeled its doors open.

Twila rolled her eyes at the misfortune of having to share the sluggish ride up with Nathan. If she *didn't*, she'd have to make several more minutes of idle — albeit *pleasant* — conversation with Jessie while she waited for the thing to make its molasses-slow return to the lobby.

Nathan hurried into the elevator. Its far glass wall faced an expansive atrium with a massive live tree surrounded by a fountain and cafeteria in the building's center. He pushed the circular indentation for the 32nd floor and rammed his fingertip into the 'door close' button.

Jessie pointed. "Best catch your ride 'less you want to enjoy my stellar company for another five minutes. You know how slow that thing is."

"Yeah," Twila agreed begrudgingly and shuffled toward the elevator. "Hold the elevator, please."

Nathan didn't budge. He glanced at her and returned his eyes forward, focusing on nothing as the doors slid slowly closed.

Twila lunged and shot her hand through the crevice, overriding the sensor. The doors crept back into their open position. Nathan sighed quietly as she stepped inside.

"*Thanks a pant-load, Nathan,*" she growled.

He was unbothered.

Twila looked out the elevator's glass wall and then around the brass interior as the machine made its ascent. She eyed the embedded lights in the ceiling and shifted her gaze to the marbled chevrons on the elevator's floor.

Anything to avoid having to make eye contact with Nasty Nate.

Nathan glanced at the smartwatch on his wrist, held by a shiny metal band. He remained a foot away from the entrance, facing the doors, waiting for them to open to the thirty-second level.

Twila watched the floors tick away on the digital banner above the doors.

14...15...16...

She sighed, folding her arms.

Nathan shifted uncomfortably at the awkward silence and dusted remnants of snow from his thick hair.

Twila primped her hair, scrunching her curls and smoothing any flyaways from wearing her beanie.

23...24...25...

Longest elevator ride ever, Twila thought.

Her stomach growled, bouncing off the brass walls like a quiet rumble of thunder. Her eyes shot over to Nathan. His brown eyes met hers for a moment.

"Sorry. Haven't eaten anything since breakfast. Mason's bringing seven-layer dip."

He forced the most polite smirk he could muster and returned his attention to the lit-up display.

30…31…

GRNNNNNNNNNN!

MMMMRRRRNNNNN.

The elevator roared, low and horrifying.

Twila and Nathan glanced around in confusion. Their enclosure pitched, sending both startled inhabitants stumbling to the clear wall overlooking the atrium, now divided horizontally in half by the concrete foundation of the floor above.

It shuddered, vibrating Nathan and Twila before grinding to a deafening, abrupt full-halt.

They stood motionless in the stilled contraption, eyes wide with alarm.

"What the—" Nathan launched forward. He pried at the doors with his fingers, glowering angrily at the digital banner over the door. "No, no, no!"

The effort was futile. The doors weren't budging.

"*Dammit!*" Nathan slammed the toe of his dress shoe into the brass as hard as he could.

Twila clamored toward the buttons on the brushed metal plate and pressed them all, hoping one would magically make the metal box roar back to life.

"Seriously?" she growled.

Chapter 2

BWAP.

BWAP.

BWAP.

The sound of Phil's tennis ball slamming against the drywall for the thousandth time made Beth grit her teeth. If she'd had a pencil in her hand, she'd have snapped it in half in frustration.

"Would you stop that?" she grumbled to her co-worker as politely as her mouth would allow.

Phil caught the ball, holding it in fingers that reeked of marijuana from the half a joint he smoked at lunch. "Yes, ma'am."

He looked like a whipped puppy, sad gaze falling to the old smashed-in spot of off-white gum on the short pile carpet.

"You don't have to call me ma'am." Beth softly pounded a closed-fist against her forehead. "I'm sorry. I'm just a little on edge right now."

"Why?"

"Doesn't matter."

"Well, sure it does. I care. C'mon. What's stuck in your craw?" He took his feet off the desk and smacked the thighs of his filthy jeans. Torn ones covered in powders, dried paint, and motor oil. "Lay it on ol' Philly here."

"No, thank you."

"Aww, come on. I may not be good at a lot of things. But I can be a *great* listener."

Beth stared at him for a moment, sizing the man up, unsure what to make of him.

"What's troublin' you?" His head bobbled a little. He raked his scarred fingers through the graying scruff on his face.

RIIIING!

The emergency line trilled. The crimson light above flashed with urgency.

A warning beacon.

Their "bat symbol."

"Commissioner Gordon needs us!" Phil said, underestimating the closeness of the walls as he lobbed the tennis ball carelessly over his shoulder. It bounced off the surface behind him, smashing through the tiny room, tearing through the contents of their desk like a ricocheted bullet, knocking over Beth's thermos of soup on its journey.

"What the hell?!" she exclaimed.

Chicken and noodles oozed down a river of invoices like piping hot magma from an erupting volcano.

"Shit! Shit!" Beth's slightly rotund frame rose from her chair with a squeak. She batted the steaming liquid from her clothes in large, furious swipes.

Phil sucked air in through his off-white teeth and hissed. "Oof. *Sorry!*" He winced and lunged for the ringing phone, leaving Beth to attend to the mess.

"*Lift You Up* Service Center," he chirped. "Is everything okay?" He listened intently, beady eyes grazing over Beth's voluptuous ass like a jaguar sizing up a potential food source. "Mmmm-hmmmmm.

What floor is saying on the panel above the door?"

Beth turned to stare at him as she patted the stew of papers and broth with a wad of blue mechanic's disposable towels. Hunks of carrot and noodles fluttered to the dingy carpet like fall leaves, landing on the carpet stained with grease and years of tracked-in dirt.

"Gotcha. Okay, we are comin' right now. Stay calm. Don't panic. Whatever you do, don't try prying open the doors or crawling out of the roof panels. Leave that stuff for the movies, okay? We'll get you out of there safely straight away."

Another pause.

"No, sir, I was *not* aware you're the Vice President, but we will—"

Phil swung a hand in circles, hoping it would somehow make the man on the other end finish his flustered tirade quicker. He covered the phone's mouthpiece and mouthed an exaggerated apology to Beth.

Irritated, she threw down a soupy paper towel and whispered, *"I can't believe you spilled my freaking lunch!"*

"I'll buy you a bagel on the way, okay? Please! I'm sorry," he quietly replied before speaking full volume into the receiver. "Yes… yes sir. Right away. As soon as we hang up here, we are on our way."

A pause.

"Mmm-hmmm. Alright. Yep. We will have you out in a jiffy, sir. Hang tight."

Staring at the mess he'd made on the desk and floor, Phil tried to hang up the phone and missed the mounted cradle on the wall, instead hitting the cork-board near it, knocking down several push-pins and safety recall bulletins. When he saw his miscalculation, he hung it up correctly. As he did, the whole cradle yanked free and smashed down on the desk with a deafening *clang.*

"You are a klutz and a half!" Beth growled, throwing down the blue paper towels and folding her beefy arms in front of her large bosom. She was a stout woman in her late forties, squat and wide with a head full of gray-brown curls.

"Look. The building we're going to has an incredible little bakery on the ground level.

Your lunch is on me just as soon as we're done. You like lox?"

After a long, annoyed pause, she finally huffed, "Yes. I like lox."

He grinned, wide and genuine. His sly grin carved deep striations through his skin. "I *knew* it!"

Her hands slunk down by her sides.

Phil watched them, unable to keep his gaze off her bare fingers. Hope flickered behind his eyes.

No wedding ring.

"Knew what?"

"You're Jewish, aren't you?" he asked, broad smile brightening behind his gray beard.

"Yeah? So?"

"I can smell my own."

"What the hell does a Jewish woman *smell* like?"

"Guilt and matzo ball soup."

"That's," she stood for a moment, shell-shocked, "fucking *offensive.*"

He ignored what she said. "Did you have a bat mitzvah?" He plucked his coat from the rack by the door and stuffed his arms in the sleeves.

"It's none of your business if I did or not." She grabbed her infinity scarf off the desk and inspected it for remnants of spilled broth before finally putting it around her neck.

"I'm simply trying to get to know you."

"You don't need to *know* me. You need to *train* me." She tossed on her thick coat and pulled on her gloves.

"Well then, grab both tool cases in there," he pointed to the adjoining room and grinned again, "because I'm about to do *both*."

She sighed deep and heavy, walked into the next room, grabbed two bulky maintenance tool kits by their handles, and returned, nudging away an errant piece of celery with her Ugg boot so she wouldn't step on it. She offered one of the kits to Phil.

He took it, turned fast, and smashed it into the back of his rolling chair, misjudging the clearance by at least half a foot. An assortment of tools rained down onto the floor. He shuffled around on his knees, trying to pick them up, struggling with the puffy fingers of his gloves.

"Do you," she hesitated, making a sour face down at him, "need to have your eyes checked?"

"Probably wouldn't hurt." He finally stood and pointed to his scuffed thick-framed eyeglasses. "This is a real old prescription." He smiled again, plucky and indomitable, and held his arm out for hers. "Shall we, *madame?*"

She scoffed and breezed past him, shuffling out the door and into the chilled city air.

Chapter 3

Nathan took a deep breath to calm himself, inhaling Twila's sweet perfume. There were subtle notes of jasmine and orange in between wafts of her fruit-scented shampoo. The faint scent of apples drew him in like a cartoon character coaxed by beckoning pie steam.

It was going to be torture to be stuck in here with *her*.

Smelling like *that*.

Looking sexy even despite her hideous Christmas sweater...

His clean-shaven jaw flexed in frustration.

Twila's eyes followed the lines of his neck down. Taut, smooth, and strong. Standing this close to the parka-clad Adonis made her whole body buzz.

How can you loathe someone so much and want to tear their clothes off simultaneously?

It was the sentiment she felt every time they were in the board room together, butting heads on ad spend and potential areas for dial-backs.

She hated that her body betrayed her like this, reacting with gooseflesh and budding warmth to his honeyed voice. Feeling even the most subtle desire whenever they were in close proximity.

Twila snapped back to reality, sobered by the concept of being suspended thirty-two floors above the ground in a malfunctioning box.

Plus…

Nathan was completely off-limits.

Fool me once; shame on you.

Fool me twice…

Chapter 4

"Why are they playing this Christmas crap so damned loud? I feel like I'm at a friggin' concert!" Meredith yelled to no one in particular. She stuffed her Secret Santa gift on the card table next to the others, crinkling the tablecloth made of wrapping paper beneath. Her eyes fixed on the various shapes and papered designs of the others. One was in a decorative bag. One was obviously a handle of booze.

One looked like a giant baby rattle…

She couldn't draw her eyes away.

"You made it. I didn't think you'd come." Laura's sweater was ornately stitched in black-and-neon-green threads in the design of a large xenomorph from the *Alien* franchise. "I dig your shirt, Meredith. That shit is *hideous*. It's gotta be between you, Caleb, and Mason for ugliest."

Meredith snapped back out of her trance for a moment. "Thanks. It was my grandmother's. She wore it un-ironically for many years."

Laura laughed and habitually swept a length of hair with choppy highlights over her shoulder. "I like it."

"Why are they playing this Christmas crap so *loud?*" Meredith grimaced at the sound of festive tunes as they blasted through the small space.

"Not sure. It was like this when I got here. This whole party is janky A.F. You seen James yet? That fucker's a menace."

"No. I didn't think he was coming now that he's allegedly on the wagon. Too many triggers."

"Oh Lord no. He's no longer on the wagon. That jerk's done fallen off, gotten tangled in the reins, and is being *dragged* by the aforementioned wagon now."

Meredith motioned to the mic stand before her on the makeshift stage. "What's this for? Please, say he's not gonna karaoke."

"You *know* he doesn't pass up any opportunity to be the center of attention. You remember what he did last year, right?"

Meredith's eyes met Laura's, but she didn't smile.

"You didn't see? He got so drunk he took his *pants* off and waved 'em overhead like a helicopter," Laura chuckled, deriving a bit of satisfaction from being the one to tell Meredith first.

"*Eww.*"

"...And his underwear was tight. Like, *real* tight."

"*Gross.*" Meredith scraped her tongue along her upper-row of teeth and made a face like she was trying to expel a mouthful of rancid food.

"There was…" Laura swallowed hard for dramatic effect, "*shrinkage.*"

"No!"

"Yeahhhh, it looked like one of those mushroom things you jump on in the Mario games. All cap. No shaft. Ton of just… *balls.*"

"Jesus, you must be *scarred.*"

"Dan, the H.R. guy, told James if he wanted to come to the party this year, suspenders were mandatory."

"He's got to be a major thorn in Dan's side. Everyone here's complained about him to Human Resources at *least* once."

"Like I said. *Menace.*"

Meredith's gaze fell and, for a few moments, she stared listlessly at a fly doing a panicked backstroke in the faux-crystal bowl of punch.

Finally, she spoke. "You think this is spiked?"

"Shit, if James is here, he's probably straight-up *roofied* the damned thing already. *Don't* drink it." Laura reached into her oversized purse, a leather pouch so full Meredith wouldn't have been surprised if it held classified documents for the FBI among the clutter within, each redacted and encased in a brown folio.

The clinking mess within her bag sounded above the *My Chemical Romance* Christmas cover, oozing loudly through the speakers flanking the makeshift stage behind her.

"Who'd you get?" Laura swung her head toward the table stuffed with gifts, still swishing through the perfumes, hairbrushes, and lipsticks in search of something.

"It's not exactly a *secret* Santa if I tell, is it?" Meredith said, voice and mind miles away amid the random bursts of loud cheers and raucous festivities in the adjoining room.

Seconds later, Laura pulled out two nips of espresso vodka. "Aha!" She unscrewed the first cap and offered it to Meredith, who promptly waved it away like poison.

"Nah. That's not a good idea."

"Oh, come on. You're not on the *clock*, Mer. Live a little!"

"I… *can't*." There was something more to her words but Laura seemed oblivious to any subtext.

"You on the wagon, too, or something?"

"Or… something."

Laura chugged the tiny open bottle and winced at the taste as she swallowed. She tossed the container at the wall and bank-shot the refuse into the mesh trashcan nearby. "Fuck! Should have gone *pro*. Could have given *Jordan* a run for his money. Surely, I'm Bulls material through and through."

Meredith cracked the slightest hint of a smile before it dissipated again.

"Jesus, Mer, it's a party. *Lighten up*. You wanna dance? Believe me when I tell you this… I *twerk* even better than I *dunk*."

Meredith shook her head. Only then did Laura glimpse the faintest welling of tears in her co-worker's eyes. She bolted forward with concern. "Whoa… hun, what's wrong?"

Laura dropped the other tiny booze bottle back in her leather void with straps and thrust herself at Meredith in an attempt to force her into a hug.

Meredith dodged artfully backward. "No, don't." She blotted her eyes with her sweatered wrists and looked around.

Becca approached with a bored look on her face and a red solo cup in hand. Her sweater was black with a bright gold swooping emblem knitted into the front with the words *Wu-Tang Clan* emblazoned across the front. "Jesus, Laura, why are you over here making people cry?"

Laura stared at Becca, wide-eyed and stupefied, unsure of how to respond to the question herself.

Becca dunked her cup in the crimson punch and shoveled out a container full. She licked the dripping liquid off the back of her hand.

The other two looked at her as if she were an android.

"*What?*"

"Most people would use the provided ladle." Laura scoffed.

Meredith had stopped crying at the bizarre sight of Becca lapping at her own wrist like a thirsty kitten.

"Oh geez. Y'all act like I have *leprosy* or something. I washed my *hands*."

"When?" Laura pressed a fist into her hip.

"Like… recently!" Becca shook her head and chewed on the side of her red cup, gnawing like a teething puppy. "*Fairly* recently," she growled, mouth full of plastic.

"How drunk are you?" Laura squinted.

Becca pried her affixed eyes from the karaoke mic on the stage behind Meredith. "…Why?"

"On a scale from Robert Downey Jr. To David Hasslehoff, how friggin' wasted are you right now?"

"We talkin' Downey *now*… or in the *80s?*"

"*Now*, dill-weed. As in sober."

"Right now? I'd say I'm rockin' a solid Amy Winehouse."

"Jesus Christ." Laura shook her head. "Drink some water."

"What? Why?! It's a party! I'm not driving!"

Laura stepped to her. "Becca, you are the only person I've ever had working under me who can actually fucking *count to thirty* in that God-forsaken inventory room. I swear, if you get so plastered tonight, you lose your job and make me have to train *another* fucking cock-sicle to take your place, I will find out where you live, and make you regret the day you were born."

"*Dan-iel!*" Becca screamed, tattling like a six-year-old child on a naughty sibling.

Daniel galloped toward them playfully. His sweater was black and gray with the image of a man with a Tommy gun and banners of block words that said, '*Keep the change ya filthy animal!*'

Caleb, a blond man with thick-rimmed military-style glasses and a sinewy physique, trailed behind him.

"Did I just hear my name?" Daniel asked, bursting with flamboyant energy.

Laura's grimace morphed into a fake smile. "No. I don't think so."

"I did," Becca stuck her tongue out at Laura.

"Dope shirt!" Caleb chimed in, staring at Becca's chest. "*Wu-Tang Clan ain't nothin' to fuck with!*" he barked, showing his age and maturity. The women jolted back a half-step as Caleb whipped his hands to form a bastardized attempt at a gang sign. "Aww man, I shoulda dressed like *Method Man!*"

The lame Caucasian shot out his hand to shake hers. "Have we met yet? I'm Caleb, sales rep for the Sports Injury division."

Becca begrudgingly shook his hand. Her expression turned sour. "Eww, dude, why is your hand all wet?"

Slightly embarrassed, Caleb wiped his palms on his own hideous sweater, one with a knitted Santa Claus making it rain presents from atop a neon unicorn standing in for Rudolph. "Sorry about that. Yeah, it's sweat."

Becca stared at her hand like it was covered in poison.

"I'm dying in this, man. I feel like it's a million degrees." Caleb dabbed the moisture on his forehead with the arm of his shirt.

"So? Take it off," Laura barked.

"No *way*. I'm *winning* that damned prize. Last year, it was two $500 gift cards. This year, I heard it's a bike."

"What are you, *twelve?* The hell do you need a bike for?" Laura sassed.

"No, like an electric one. With a motor!" Caleb's jaw hung slack, shocked at how utterly unimpressed she was. "Those are like *two thousand bucks!*"

"This is *Manhattan,* dude!" Laura didn't hesitate to tear into the man she'd only just been introduced to. "Have you *been* on the streets of this town? People don't *stop* for bikes. And on top of it, you gotta dodge all those damned pedestrians and *LunchMunch* delivery guys? Hmm-nnnn. No thanks. I'm a subway rider." She folded her arms and stomped a foot, swinging her head around to stare at Meredith. "I'll be so *pissed* if it's a lame-ass bike!"

"So, what'd you call me over for?" Daniel asked, looking less-than-impressed and cocking a hip out in the most dramatic way possible.

Laura stared at Becca with a smug look that said, 'Tell him.'

Becca shrugged, "Laura is trying to mother me."

"No, I'm trying to cut her off. She's plastered." Scowling, Laura grabbed a cookie from the platter on the table, and annihilated it in three large bites.

"I'm an adult! And I'm not driving" Becca growled, shaking her solo cup at him.

"Well, there shouldn't be any booze here," he laughed, nerves starting to fray from attempting to keep the celebratory gaggle of misfits in line, "I asked the higher-ups to make *sure* this was a dry party."

Laura's eyes drifted to the bowl of punch that was certainly spiked.

"Fuckin' *lamewads*," Becca growled. Then, she threw her solo cup carelessly over her shoulder and marched off.

Daniel's brown eyebrows rose. "Remind me not to get on her bad side. Sheesh!" He adjusted his thin, wire-framed glasses and shook his head.

Laura grumbled, flicking one of the presents on the Secret Santa table so hard with her middle finger that she ripped a small hole in the paper. She pulled her hand back and tried to play it cool. Just then, Lester, a stout Puerto Rican woman with a shoulder-length mop of curls and a substantial frame, burst through a nearby door with a mischievous smile.

Out of breath, Lester doubled over, like a linebacker during a time out. Her accent was thick. "Jesus, that is too many floors! Why does this place have to be so high up?"

Lester huffed a few more big lungfuls of air and then stood straight.

"Why didn't you take the elevator?" Laura asked, staring as if Lester had grown a third arm out of her forehead.

"I wait and… wait. The elevator… is out." She wiped a bead of sweat from the side of her face. "It wouldn't come. I wait for fifteen minutes before I take the stairs."

Daniel grabbed a fresh, red cup and dunked it in the punch, shoveling out a full container of liquid.

Meredith watched, appalled. "Doesn't anybody use a ladle?!"

Ignoring the question, Dan rushed the drink over to the wheezing newcomer. "Here, have something to drink."

Lester took the drink from Dan.

"I wouldn't—" Laura started.

But it was too late. The Puerto Rican woman greedily chugged the entire contents in one go. Meredith and Laura glanced at each other, wincing at the irony of Parramore's new head of 'Health and Personnel' downing the large helping of questionable punch like a woman in the desert dying of thirst.

Without a word, Caleb scurried off into the next room.

Breathing heavily, Lester nodded in appreciation at Daniel, crushed the cup, jumped, and launched it fifteen feet. It landed square in the trash receptacle with a gentle plastic-sounding *swish*.

Meredith looked at Laura. "Uh oh, Jordan. Someone's here to rattle your cage. Looks like Isiah Thomas is in the house."

Laura scoffed. "I don't know who that is."

"The Detroit Pistons? Michael Jordan's biggest rival?" Meredith's face scrunched.

"Is that even a real team? *The Pistons?*" Laura seemed skeptical.

"Yes," Lester interjected loudly, shocked at Laura's ignorance on the matter. Her eyes landed on Meredith. Lester looked the woman up and down slowly and then winked.

Meredith's smile faded, and she cupped her mouth. She took off running for the bathroom.

Daniel and Laura stood in stunned silence.

"Eh, it's okay," Lester cracked her neck like a glow stick and shrugged off the slight, no longer affected by Meredith's obvious disgust. "Sometimes, I have this effect on women."

Lester unzipped her leather jacket, and as soon as she pried the lapels apart, Laura cried out. "Awww, Lord! There goes the frickin' contest."

"What?" Dan looked confused.

Laura motioned to Lester's sweater, one irreverently depicting a knitted version of Keanu Reeves swathed in a Christ-like robe. He had a golden halo of light around his head and held a black puppy lovingly in his arms.

Laura approached and pursed her lips. "I hope you enjoy your *stupid* electric bike."

With that, she stormed off into the next room, the contents of her purse jingling with every step.

"Bike? What is she talking about, this… electric bike?" Lester asked.

Daniel shrugged. "Some people think that might be the prize this year."

"I hope not. I ride the *subway*. I don't need none of this bike." Lester placed her jacket over the back of a nearby folding chair. "Where is the... all of the *hot* women?" She asked genuinely, her English broken.

Daniel chuckled nervously. "Now, Lester, you know I'm *H.R.*, right?"

"What is this H.R.? Does it stand for hair removal?" She aggressively rubbed his bald head like a school bully and cackled.

He took a deep breath with his eyes closed and whispered, *"Woosah,"* before smoothing his remaining few sprigs of dishwater-blond hair. When he opened his eyes, he pretended he hadn't heard her last comment. "Nice seeing you, Lester. I'm going to go find Mason."

"Wait," Lester hollered behind him and he stopped in his tracks, "is anyone in this office a, like a, *lesbian?*" She smiled and rubbed her hands together.

Daniel craned his neck around to look at her, appalled.

"Of course... I mean," she laughed, "other than *me?*"

"I... have... no idea." Daniel didn't blink. "Do you *really* not know what H.R. means?"

"No."

"It means," he turned to face her, "Human Relations."

"Okay. Good." It was clear those words meant absolutely nothing to her. "That is what I am looking for, too! Yes, I do need some *human relations*, too." She flashed a sideways grin at him and then she gasped. "I brought mistletoe!" She pulled a mangled piece of it out of her tight pants pocket. "Look, I don't need to find the office, uh, Mother *Mary*. I am looking for the more of a Mary *Magdalene*."

He snatched the sprig of mistletoe from her, stomped across the room, and chucked it in the trash.

"No! *Bad Lester.*" Daniel shamed her like an obnoxious dog. "No *mistletoe* and no Mary *Magdalenes*. This is company property and, look, I get it. I'm a cool guy. But don't make me write you up." He made an exaggerated disappointed expression and pointed a finger, "*Behave.*"

"Jeesh, yes, sir." She stepped back, palms out.

Daniel stormed off, shaking his head.

Lester retrieved the gnarled mistletoe from the trash and tapped it in her hand. "Now… Where is this… my little ho, ho, *ho?*"

"Breathe *in*," Nathan instructed, kneeling beside Twila, soothing her body's desire to hyperventilate. "*Aaaaand* breathe out."

Twila did as she was told, peering into Nathan's intense, earth-brown eyes as he softly caressed the back of her hand to comfort her. Despite the metal box they were in being jammed tightly in place, the world felt like it was spinning at his touch.

"Just focus on me," he directed.

Twila expelled another long, deep breath and slid her hand away from him. This was Nasty Nate, the cold curmudgeon with convenient amnesia. "I think I'm alright now."

Nathan looked at the floor, legs aching from kneeling beside her for so long. He lowered himself slowly to the floor, using his folded coat as a seat cushion. Despite the lumpiness, it was better than sitting on the dirty floor like Twila was. He removed the large cashmere scarf still around his neck and placed it in the corner, fully-revealing the hideous, brown-and-green argyle sweater with its busy, mustard-yellow diamond pattern.

"Oh, wow. I didn't think you'd be joining the festivities," Twila managed, leaning her head against the shiny wall behind her.

"I'm afraid I don't follow."

"The ugly sweater contest. You were gonna enter, too?"

He glanced down at his shirt and frowned. "*No*, I was just going to make some announcements while everyone was gathered, but now I know to burn this *sweater*. So… thanks for *that*."

Twila winced. "Sorry."

Nathan settled against the wall and sighed.

"Got any big plans tonight then?" Twila asked, searching for a distraction with idle chit-chat.

He shrugged. "I wouldn't say big."

"Care to elaborate?"

"No," he said curtly.

"*Alright.*" Her mouth snapped shut for a long moment. Finally, it opened again, tone tinged in mild frustration. "What's your father up to tonight? I'm sure he's not gonna be at this thing."

"No clue. I'm not my father's keeper."

Why is she pretending to care?

What the hell does she want?

Twila felt her anxiety swell but knew there was never a person she couldn't crack with a little kindness. If she had to be stuck with him in a brass cage for God knows how long, she might as well try to be friendly. "That's fair. It's like… if you asked me what my parents are doing tonight. I don't know."

Silence.

Maddening silence.

Twila crossed her arms. "Did you know Daniel the H.R. guy is having sex with Paula from accounting?"

Nathan's eyes narrowed, interest only slightly piqued. Looking into Twila's steel-blue eyes, he tried to assess her seriousness.

He studied her plump lips for any hint of a grin.

Nothing.

As she rolled her eyes and glanced out the glass wall into the atrium, Nathan's eyes followed the curve of her neck down and stole a quick glance at her sweater-clad D-cups.

As she glanced back at him, his eyes rose swift and smooth to meet hers again.

He smirked. If what she said was true, he'd have to have an uncomfortable talk about workplace fraternization with the goober running Human Resources on Monday. He could already hear all the 'Goshes' and 'Gollys' now. Dan talked like a preschool teacher.

"Where'd you hear that?" Nathan finally asked, trying to decide whether it was fact or fiction. "We have strict policies against interpersonal relationships in the office. If you're serious, I need to know."

With his authoritative tone and stern gaze, Twila felt her stomach release the butterflies that had long been locked away. "Oh, please. Policy-*shmolicy*. Workplace romances happen. If you shit-canned everyone who went on an inter-company date, you'd have like five people left. And one of them is only because Lester is the only *confirmed* lesbian at Parramore."

"So you're saying it's more of a *widespread* problem. I'll have my secretary send out a company-wide memo next week."

"No, I just meant it's a rule that can be difficult to enforce." Twila's thoughts drifted to the kiss…

Against the copier.

Hands roaming.

Breath, hot and frantic, entwining into a storm cloud of desire as clothing was shed…

Then her thoughts drifted to the innocuous jiggle of the handle followed by the knock at the locked copy room door.

…The one that halted that passionate moment for good.

"I was just kidding," she lied. Dan deserved to find love, even if he was annoying. "I was mostly just testing to see if you were listening."

He scoffed and stared up at the ceiling tiles and inlaid light fixtures. "My brain just tends to tune out white noise."

Did he just call my talking white noise?

Twila flexed her feet back and forth in front of her, following Nathan's gaze up to the lights in the ceiling, too. Bored, she closed one eye, then the other, watching the bulbs dance in place.

After a few seconds of that, she pulled out her phone and sent a text to Becca.

> **TWILA: Hey girl. You hear the news? I'm stuck in the elevator between the 31st and 32nd floors.**

A few seconds passed.

CHIRP! Twila's phone chimed a loud, obnoxious noise.

> **BECCA: What the fuck? Seriously? I need you up here!**

> **BECCA: James is already hammered. We won't be able to keep him away from the karaoke machine much longer.**

> **TWILA: God help us all.**

BECCA: Fucking shimmy up the elevator shaft if you gotta. Just get here!

TWILA: Trust me, I would if I could. I'm stuck in here with Nasty Nate.

The response was immediate.

BECCA: NOOOOOOOOOO! WHAT?!

TWILA: Yup!

BECCA: Oh my God, girl. I pity you. I wish I could hand you down some of this spiked-ass punch.

Another response came a few seconds later.

BECCA: Wait, have you tried opening the door?

TWILA: He tried already. Maintenance guys said don't

open the door and don't craw
through the ceiling tiles.

BECCA: Well there goes the
whole Die Hard concept I was
about to pitch you.

Another text message chimed. This time
from her mother.

MOM: You don't have a date
again this year for Christmas
dinner, right?

TWILA: Correct.

MOM: Okay, well Betsy, the
neighbor two houses over, her
son just came back from
overseas and he is dying to
meet you.

MOM: Shall I have you both
over for a nice Christmas lunch
on Sunday?

TWILA: We talked about this
mom.

The three dots popped up and then disappeared. They returned and disappeared yet again. Her mother was trying to word her argument to reconsider just right.

Twila shook her head and stuffed her phone back in the pocket of her coat in the corner. She rose to her feet.

She stepped to the elevator doors and dug her festive green gel-tipped nails into the crack and yanked in opposing directions.

"They said not to do that," Nathan said passively.

"I'm aware. I was right here when they told you on the intercom." She held her eyes closed tight for a moment and then spoke again. "I was just trying to see if we were close enough to the next floor to pry it open and climb out."

She stepped just a smidgen too far back in the tight space and accidentally marked Nathan's brown wingtip oxford shoes with the black sole of her sensible Mary Janes.

"Hey, these were expensive." He pulled his feet in close and scrubbed at the mark with a wet thumb.

CHIRP!

CHIRP!

Twila growled, went back to her coat, and grabbed her cell again. Two more messages from Becca.

> **BECCA: You got this.**

> **BECCA: Just think of happy shit.**

Her fingers flew over the phone's on-screen keyboard.

> **TWILA: Becca, I'm freaking out. I feel so claustrophobic. And I can't be stuck in here with rude-ass Nasty Nate.**

> **BECCA: Girl.**

> **BECCA: You're a bad bitch, not a *sad* bitch. Pull it together.**

> **BECCA: It's only... what? A few hours? Maybe less?**

The thought of being in there for several more hours made Twila want to hyperventilate all over again.

Suddenly, she heard a muffled scream sound through the door. Nate's eyes lit up.

"Can you hear me?" The words were muffled but Nate and Twila understood them immediately.

"Yes!" Twila screamed, tears of joy filling her eyes. It was Becca. She was so close. The sound brought comfort.

CHIRP!

> **BECCA: Okay. You can hear me. You're close. That's good. I'm sure the repair people well be here soon.**
>
> **BECCA: When you get out of there, I'm going to get you so drunk you won't even know what an elevator IS.**

That made Twila chuckle aloud.

> **TWILA: Thank you. <3**

**BECCA: I mean, like,
photocopy-your-tits-drunk.**

Twila laughed harder, straining to see the screen through tears.

TWILA: Deal.

**BECCA: I gotta get off this floor
before James mounts me like a
horny chihuahua.**

Not a moment after they heard the chirp of Twila's last incoming text, Becca shouted, muffled by thick layers of brass and concrete. "James, for the love of God, if you don't stop breathing down my neck, I am gonna punch you in the dick!"

Even though the confined duo couldn't see him, they could hear the alcohol-infused lust James's voice. "God, I love me a feisty woman!"

"You realize H.R. is still a thing, right?" It was Becca again. "That department doesn't just disappear because you've chugged a gallon of eggnog."

"*You've* got a department I could disappear into."

"Jesus Christ, James. I'm going to turn a damn *hose* on you!"

Twila laughed, but it slowly abated when reality set back in. *She was still stuck in an elevator with Nasty Nate.*

"Hey." Nathan finally spoke. He cleared his throat and pulled a flask from his coat pocket. "Want some?"

"What is it?"

"Whiskey."

"*Way to bury the lead.* You had that the whole time you were making me do all those deep breathing exercises?"

Nathan laughed, fighting the forming grin on his face. "Breathing is better for you. I was doing you a favor."

"Breathing is for *chumps*," she joked, extending her hand for the container.

He unscrewed the lid, took a swig, and then passed it to Twila. "Cheers."

She took it from him, fingertips grazing his during the handoff. She softened a little. "Cheers."

He huffed at the burn and shook his head at the floor. "I figured since we're stuck, might as well make the best of it."

She sniffed its contents and finally poured herself a mouthful. Her face contorted at the bitter swill. She whipped her head, tongue out, hoping air would help the sting. "Ugh! Why does it burn so much?"

He snickered at her reaction and waved for her to give it back.

She's kind of adorable.

"Gah! I think that stuff's gone bad."

"It doesn't go bad. This is forty-five year old whiskey. Top shelf."

"Tastes like battery acid."

"Go around licking batteries often?"

Twila flashed a smug look with narrowed eyes and then licked the back of her hand in an attempt to get the awful taste out of her mouth.

Nathan laughed. "Oh, come on, it's not that bad."

Nathan smiled and took another swallow. Twila watched his face remain expressionless as he swallowed, studying his hardened, attractive features. Perfect bone structure.

Carefully-styled hair. Soft eyes with thick lashes…

She straightened her posture and looked away the moment she realized she was staring.

"Another?" He offered it to her again.

She stared at his extended hand for a moment, imagining how it would feel against her skin…

Sliding between her thighs…

Suddenly, she perked up and her eyes met his. "Sure." She took it. "If we're gonna be stuck in here together, might as well have a little fun while we're in here."

The comment caught him by surprise. *Did she mean that as flirtatious as it sounded?*

Twila unscrewed the cap and took another drink, trying to skip her tongue altogether and toss the vile liquid to the back of her throat so she wouldn't have to taste it. The first sip hit her empty stomach like a fireball, warming her from the inside out. She smiled.

"That time, you took it like a pro." Nathan held a hand up to high-five her. She smacked it but the two held their palms together for a split second after, neither wanting to pull away from the other. Finally, Twila's hand retreated and the heat from her stomach rose to her blushing cheeks.

The elevator felt sweltering and the cooled metal and glass around them offered little relief.

Twila scooted away from him, toward the windowed wall overlooking the atrium. There was nowhere in the elevator to go to get away from the deliciously woodsy undertones of Nathan's intoxicating cologne.

From opposing sides of the elevator, they offered shy glances as the deafening silence took up residency between them.

Chapter 6

Twila's face and neck blushed from the alcohol. Ever the lightweight, the liquid social lubricant coursed through her veins, settling in her gurgling stomach.

"So… what department do you work for again?" Nathan asked, trying to make awkward conversation.

"Are you… serious?" Twila frowned

"I mean, I know I've seen you in board meetings, but I can't seem to remember what you do. You're, like, one of the accountants, right?"

Her face morphed from hurt to pissed-off in a nanosecond. She had to fight hard to keep her words from coming out sopping with vitriol. "Nathan, I'm Parramore's financial

Advisor. I've counseled your father for like six years now. You seriously…"

Twila was flabbergasted.

How the hell does he not know all I've done for this company by now?!

Nathan looked at his shoes and back at her, his tone defensive. "Don't take it personally—"

"It's kinda hard not to," she growled. "Do you even know my name?"

"Twila."

"Well," she scoffed and looked away, "color *me* surprised."

"What's my last name?" Her hurt eyes flashed like blue streaks back in his direction.

"Hen," his eyebrow raised, "son? No, Hen-der-son?"

"Is that your final answer?" Her tone was curt.

"I'd like to phone a friend, actually."

"Pfft. You are the weakest link." She looked away again and folded her arms over her chest. "*Goodbye.*"

"I'm sorry. I talk to a lot of people in a day and see so many people in those damned board room meetings. Do you think I know all of their names?"

"No, but I'd expect that the people who *advise you* on what your company does with its money *should* matter."

Frustrated, he sighed and pressed his lips together.

She glared at him. She wasn't sure if it was the heat in the claustrophobic space, the alcohol, or the agitation, but her blood was boiling. Her sweater now felt torturous, like the confining walls of a toaster oven, broiling her alive with a sudden flash of sweltering heat.

She fanned herself with her hand.

"It's fucking hot in here, right?" he asked, trying to smooth things over between them.

She didn't respond.

He leaned forward and grabbed the hem of his argyle sweater, ripping the thick article over his head, dragging the t-shirt beneath up with it and exposing half of his abdomen. He tossed the sweater into a rumpled ball on the floor and looked up at her, raven-black hair mussed and staticky.

Twila wanted to laugh at the sight of his wild tresses looking crazy for once. He always seemed like the type who wouldn't be caught dead in front of someone with so much as a hair out of place.

But she didn't dare laugh. She needed him to know that she was still fucking livid at his apparent amnesia.

But a moment later, she caught herself thinking about his exposed skin again, replaying that recent moment in her head like a favorite song on a mental mix tape.

Nathan didn't have a "desk body." Now that he was down to just a plain white tee, she could see he was all muscle. She'd fantasized as much in the years since they'd met. Though he was always polished in suits and button-downs, he used to sport polos, ones that pulled in all the right places to subtly advertise the pecs and washboard abs beneath.

Now, as Twila ogled his physique, another primal flash of heat traveled across the tender flesh of her throat, down through her torso, and lingered long and hard between her thighs.

The sight of his toned stomach awakened her nerve endings, turning her thoughts for him into something innately sexual.

The things she wished she could do to him flashed like an erotic slideshow and her mind reeled from the endless possibilities.

If only he wasn't such a dick…

"I'm sorry you're upset," he said, positioning his back to the brass wall and staring up at the ceiling tiles again.

"I'm not upset. I'm just… shocked," she muttered.

"Why is it such a big deal to you?"

"It doesn't matter."

Nathan prodded. "Clearly, it does."

"I can't read minds, alright? We're both adults last time I checked." Nathan watched her pert lips press into an agitated line.

"So you don't remember?"

"Remember what?"

She looked away, disgusted.

"What the hell is *wrong* with you?"

"We kissed, alright?" She shouted it far louder than she'd intended. Her chest ached with embarrassment and humiliation. The memory she had of his soft lips fervently pressed against hers in the copy room two Christmases ago felt ridiculous now.

Their make-out session had left her with little more than a pair of soaked panties and nights of frustrated longing.

"Two years ago? At the Christmas party?" Her voice was high. She could see from the blank expression on his face that none of this information was clicking for him. Seeing him blank out over the best kiss of her life made her want to cry. She fought the tears, unwilling to let him have the satisfaction.

"What are you talking about?"

"Okay. Fine. Play dumb."

"I'm not playing dumb. I don't remember."

"We were drunk on eggnog. We were talking for a bit. You grabbed me by the hand and pulled me into the copy room," she paused to let it sink in. When it didn't, she continued, "It was back just before you became Vice President."

Nothing still.

Just a blank look.

Twila's voice cracked. "You pushed me against the copier and we made out.

Remember? And someone knocked so we composed ourselves. You said you wanted to see me again. I gave you my number… is this just all a complete blank to you?"

"Twila half that party is a black spot on my memory. My grandfather died the day before and I got absolutely *shitfaced* at that party. I was pre-gaming before I even got into the *building*. I *arrived* wasted, Twila. I don't remember *any* of that and I sure as hell don't remember getting anyone's *number*."

He thought back all of those hazy parties, back in the days before he had so much crushing responsibility. His mouth opened and then shut again.

Neither of them spoke.

Defeated, he finally sighed. "I think you're thinking of someone else. You're fucking gorgeous. I'd remember if we kissed."

The compliment warmed her, despite her frustration. Suddenly, she wished she, too, had the foresight to wear an undershirt beneath her sweater.

After a long pause, Twila finally spoke.

"If you don't believe me, check your phone."

Nathan pulled out his phone and opened the thumbnail for his contacts.

He hung his head in shame, glanced into her oceanic eyes, and then allowed his gaze to fall back to those words burning through the screen.

There it was.

Twila-fucking-Henderson.

Shit.

Chapter 7

"Well, Twila is stuck in the damned elevator," Becca said, sighing and lobbing her cell phone on her desk.

"No!" Leonard exclaimed, using his dirty shoes to push himself back further than his ergonomic chair should ever lean. His sweater bore Rudolph in board shorts and sunglasses, sipping a mai tai on a sunny beach. To add to the atrocity, red glitter-doused bows were sewn onto the knitted pattern at random.

"Yup. You'll never guess who she's stuck in there with either," Becca said, sucking down the contents of one of the mini booze bottles Laura had just handed out like Santa's drunken elf.

"Who?" Mason sounded vaguely interested as he lifted his head from his desk.

He took another long chug of eggnog from his cup and propped his head up lazily on his palm.

"*Nasty Nate.*" Becca rolled her eyes and stared at the ceiling. "God help her."

"He's not such a bad guy," Leonard said, swirling the ice in his water with a finger.

"Bull*shit*," Becca snapped. "He's such a tool."

"No, he isn't."

"He fired Zach over nothing. Right before Christmas!"

Mason giggled into the stack of invoices and sales reports beneath him.

"What's so funny?" Becca hissed and then balanced the point of a pencil on the desk carefully by the eraser. With her other hand, she flicked the hell out of it, launching the wooden projectile across the room like a missile.

Then she set up another.

"Dude, Zach didn't get fired over *nothing*." Mason's voice was muffled. He could smell the noxious combo of booze, vanilla, and milk from his breath, blowing back onto his own face.

Leonard was laughing now, too. Arms crossed, he bobbed the chair slowly until one of the five feet left the floor in a sketchy display of balance and coordination.

"The fuck are *you* laughing at, putz?" She shifted in her chair, aiming the pencil for Mason now.

"Zach got fired for bangin' *Meredith* in the copy room."

"Bull*shit.*"

"You haven't heard about all that?! Where the hell have you been, Becca?"

"In the stock room! Doing *inventory!* Dammit, man, that place is like a fucking *dead zone* for gossip." She shot the pencil at him. The point hit him in the shoulder like a lame arrow before trickling pathetically to the ground.

She set up another and winced. "Meredith and *Zach?* Ewwww."

"Yup," Leonard finally chimed in, flashing a pearly set of white teeth that contrasted beautifully with his dark skin, which looked almost like veneers. "I didn't believe it at first, either."

"I ain't buyin' it." Becca flicked the pencil again and smacked Mason right on the back of his head with it.

He mumbled into the desk, "Are you quite finished?"

Out of pencils now, Becca loaded a Sharpie marker up to do the same, never acknowledging him. "Meredith is so mousy, and Zach is like… all bravado."

"Opposites attract." Mason burped, wet and nasty.

"Dude, Meredith would be punching above her weight class. Zach had like a damned twelve-pack."

"When did you see him shirtless?" Leonard asked it fast, pitch high.

"St. Patty's Day last year. We all went to McDougherty's for green beers, and he ended up having so many that he took his shirt off and whirled it like a lasso at the female bartender."

She flicked the marker, and it smacked Mason with an audible *thunk*.

"Ow! Fucking stop! Jesus, you remind me of my little sister." Mason hurled a cup of pens at her. The mesh container and all of its contents scattered.

"So, did they get caught?" Becca stopped flicking them now. Instead, she grabbed another off the floor and immaturely lobbed it straight at him.

Leonard bobbled in his chair again and laughed. "Fucking Nate walked in there to get some fucking forms he printed for that new hire, the lesbian chick," he snapped his fingers, "Oh shit. What's her name?"

"Lester?"

"Yeah, Lester. So he goes in, and there's Zach. He's got Meredith bent over the copier, just goin' to town on her. We're talkin' balls-deep."

"*Dubious.*" She didn't believe it. "If that's true, how come Zach got fired and Meredith didn't?"

"Oh, she *almost* did. She's on probation. But Daniel was worried that it might be an H.R. nightmare if she said it wasn't consensual or something, so she got off with a warning."

"Plus," Mason slurred, "this wasn't Zach's first offense. A month ago, he got caught smoking a fucking bowl in the janitorial closet by the cleaning staff."

"Oof." Becca made a sour face.

Chapter 8

"Honey, are you gonna come out of there?" Laura cooed through the stall door.

"*Yes*, please, sweetheart. *You* gotta come out." Lester's accent held strong. "I have to *pee*. There is only the one stall."

The room echoed with the sound of Meredith retching into the toilet again. Lester stepped back from the stall and frowned. Then, she looked at Laura, eyed her up and down, and flashed a flirtatious smile, arching one eyebrow.

"Cool your jets, I'm straight."

"So is the spaghetti… until it gets *wet*." Lester took a slow, calculated step closer to Laura and leaned a shoulder against the wall near a hand dryer. She pulled the mangled mistletoe out of her pants pocket and tapped it in her palm. "Eh? What do you say?"

Lester held the mistletoe above Laura's blonde head and smiled.

Laura rolled her eyes and ping-ponged over to the sink, away from the woman. She shook her head and mouthed, "*Not a damn chance.*"

"Laura? I'm… scared." Meredith's voice rose above the metal barrier separating them, small and meek, like a frightened child.

"I'm sure it's just a bug. You know people always pick up nasty shit around the holidays because of all the get-togethers and weather and stuff."

"It's… not a bug!" Meredith sobbed. Her hisses echoed, using the bowl as a miniature amphitheater.

Suddenly, there was a shuffling noise, and the door creaked slowly open. Meredith dabbed her wet mouth against her wrist and wiped her mascara-smeared eyes. "I'm pregnant, Laur."

Laura and Lester stood in stunned silence at the admission. Meredith dove head-first, burying her face in Laura's *Alien* sweater.

"Awww, no. Don't you cry," Lester said.

Meredith spun in Laura's arms and sniffled, staring at the new co-worker with a wrecked face.

Lester held up the mistletoe again, this time over Meredith.

"Eh? What do you say? One little smooch for the holidays?"

Meredith stared at the woman like she had five heads. "Lester… you just heard me *puking* in there."

Lester let out an exasperated sigh and chucked the mistletoe in the trash. She barged into the vacant stall, slammed the door, and loudly unzipped her leather pants.

As she pissed, she spoke again. "These New Yorkers is all the same. *Ay-yay-yay…*"

Chapter 9

Nathan's phone flashed a low battery symbol that blinked away, showing the text on the screen.

DAVID CARSON: When can we get together to discuss some of our new products? We just patented a revolutionary new design for the end of the plunger on hypodermics that you are going to want to see.

DAVID CARSON: Merry Christmas, btw.

Nathan locked the screen and lolled his head back against the brass.

"I'm sorry," he offered weakly. "I didn't mean to lead you on like that."

Twila's shoulders sank. "I didn't care that you lead me on. I just… I don't know… I liked how you made everyone feel important and worth knowing in those days. You used to ask about people's kids and send sympathy cards. You were this attractive powerhouse." The words spewing from her buzzed mouth surprised her. It was too late. She couldn't take them back. "But now you're a bit of a curmudgeon."

"*Curmudgeon?*"

"Yeah it means—"

"Oh, I know what it means. I just haven't heard anyone use that term since, like, the *90s.*"

"The point is, you used to be this cool, casual guy. You were the life of the whole office back when I started. Now," she hesitated for a moment and then blurted, "you're a stick in the mud. You're all business all the time. And, then, last week, when you fired Zach…"

"What about it?" His tone was defensive. His body flexed and he sat rigid as if he were about to be attacked.

"Did you *have* to do that during the holidays? In front of everyone?"

"Yes, Twila. I can't have people having *sex* on company property. I had no choice!" Nathan sighed and scrubbed his dark eyebrows with the pads of his fingers, looking stressed. "I can't be the same person I was because *life* isn't the same as it was. I don't know how all of this is supposed to work in your *idealistic mind,* but that *is* how life works for the *rest* of us. Being VP comes with great responsibilities. I'm sorry, but co-worker friendships are not my concern. Running a profitable company *is*. Selling bulk bandages to Mount Sinai is. Making sure the right shipment of Bledsoe boots makes it to Secaucus, *that* is what keeps me up at night. Not giving some sales rep who can't keep his *dick* in his pants the axe too close to Christmas."

She used all the restraint she could muster to choke back her rage. "A job doesn't change who you *are*. It doesn't define you. Your *actions* define you. You've changed. You've forgotten who you are. Hell, you've forgotten who *we* are. *Literally*. And…" she looked flustered, whirling her hands before slapping them onto her thighs, "apparently, our kiss… wasn't worth remembering."

She looked away, deflated.

He shook his head, scoffed, and ran his fingers through his mussed hair. "I'm sorry about the kiss, alright? I feel like a real asshole right now about that." He sighed. "And maybe you're right. As far as who I *used* to be… look, I don't take *joy* in firing people. It's the worst. I still care about our workers, but I don't have the time to spend twenty minutes listening to Tom in advertising bitch about his wife and kids, or look at Laura's vacation pictures."

"She's going to Cancun next," she interjected.

"Is she?" He rolled his eyes and softened a bit. "Lucky her."

Silence.

Then, he spoke again.

"Feels like every moment of my day is spoken for. I can barely take a piss without my administrative assistant having a coronary. Dad's checked out. He's ready to retire and hand me the reigns. He's never fucking around any more. So shit doesn't get done on a higher level around here unless I do it."

Seeing the grave expression etched into his face, she felt a pang of sympathy.

"You're right. I don't know anything about the kind of stress you must be under. And, for what it's worth, there are plenty of us here who care about you as a person."

Nathan fidgeted nervously with his hands.

"And the kiss… it's in the past. I shouldn't have even brought it up." She hugged her legs to her chest, resting her chin on her knees.

Nathan saw the disappointment in her eyes and felt the insatiable urge to take it all away. He desperately wanted to go back to that night…

To bring her intense satisfaction instead of remorseful regret.

To fill the black hole in his memory with the taste of her lips on his, savoring every bit of her…

To let his hands wander the warm curves of her incredible body…

To make her gasp and touch her tenderly, intimately, in all of the places that would take her breath away.

Chapter 10

"Wow, I'm outta shape," Beth huffed, doubling over on the landing of an endless set of stairs. "This kinda stuff really makes you realize how much we take lifts for granted."

"Yeah, Beth, I don't wanna tell you how many flights we have left," Phil chewed his lower lip, one dry from the harsh winter weather.

"What do you mean? We're almost there. You said they're stuck between thirty-one and thirty-two."

Silence swept through the stair-filled column for a moment. The only thing making noise was the washing-machine-like hum of dozens of tube lights washing the off-white walls with their garish yellow beams and the pair of the sweating maintenance worker's jingling heavy tool bags.

"Look, I don't want to kill the morale here—"

"Kill the morale? I just climbed four thousand steps to get here. How you gonna kill morale more than *that?*" Beth set her tool bag down on the next landing and glared at Phil.

He was half her weight and had a good ten years on her. He had no doubt she could snap him like a twig if she wanted to. He swallowed hard. "Well, don't be mad… but this building is fifty-six stories."

"Um, so?"

"So… the machine rooms are at the *top* of the building. To check the motor, we have to go up there. And God forbid we need any parts not in these bags—"

"So, what you're saying is, we aren't even halfway up yet?"

"Correct." He nodded and plucked a pack of cigarettes out of the breast pocket of his flannel shirt. Using the hand carrying his tool bag, he fished a lighter out of his filthy pants pocket and lifted it to his mouth. As he did, the open tool pouch tipped sideways, and three wrenches slid out with ease, tumbling down through the center gap in the stairwell like a metal hailstorm. He jolted, spilling screwdrivers and miscellaneous tools onto the steps between Beth and him.

"Take cover below!" he screamed at the top of his lungs, dropping his cigarette down the gap. It careened down in the slow gravitational free-fall in the wake of the wrenches.

His heart pounded louder than the sound of the faraway metal clattering to the concrete thirty stories down. The sound rang quietly through the tense air.

"You could have just fucking murdered somebody!" Beth screamed, picking up a screwdriver and threatening to throw it at him. She halted just before she launched it, knowing it, too, could be a deadly projectile if it fell.

Phil looked at her, eyes wide enough behind his thick glasses that both of his entire, dulled irises were on full display, mouth agape in shock and horror. "What the hell just happened?"

"You went to light up a cancer stick, and your clumsy ass dropped a bunch of tools!"

"I'm aware." His voice sounded calm.

"Then why did you *ask?*"

He swallowed hard, hunched down, and collected the array of items on the steps in front of him.

"Is everyone okay down there?" Beth screamed toward the first floor, her voice echoing off the hard walls.

Silence.

Electrical humming.

No response.

"If it hit someone, I doubt they'd be responding, Bethany."

She growled. "It's Beth, alright? Not Bethany. I don't go around calling you *Phillip*. And you're being awful *lax* about this!"

"I feel like you're coming at me a little hot right now. Need I remind you that I am your superior and that you are still in your probationary period?"

"Need I remind you that you could have just *murdered* someone? *And* that you spilled my soup earlier? That was my *lunch*, Phil. You wanna know why I'm coming at you hot right now? I'm *hangry*. My legs are *burning*. My bubbe's in the hospital. And instead of being with her, I'm here, in a stairwell with the clumsiest fuckin' guy in Manhattan." She scoffed. "Oh! And I just found out I'm only halfway to the top of this damn building."

"Look, I'm sorry about the soup, okay? I promise. Once we get this schmuck out of the elevator, I'll take you to that bagel place. I promise, you've never had a lox this good in your *life*. The salmon is so fresh, you'd swear they just plucked it out of the Hudson five minutes ago."

He pulled another cigarette out of his pack, set his tools down on a step, and lit it carefully this time. He took a deep drag, picked up his bag, and motioned to the next set of stairs with his head.

"C'mon. Let's get a move on. Sooner we're done, the sooner you get smoked fish and capers in your belly."

Beth trudged behind him with reluctance. "If we need whatever you dropped later, I'm not going down there to get it. I'm just saying that *right* friggin' now."

Phil chuckled and blew out a lungful of smoke. "Fair enough."

After another long silence, he finally spoke again.

"So, Beth…"

"Yes, Phil," she grumbled taking every step harder than the last.

"Pretty gal like you got a fella?"

Beth could only laugh.

Chapter 11

Phil and Beth breathed heavily, thighs burning as they reached the top landing. The weight of their tool bags and shed outerwear felt like it had tripled on the grueling walk up.

Phil laughed as he gripped the handrail, breathing hard. Sweat followed the deep lines of his skin like slow-running water through a cracked rock face.

"Did I tell ya' I nearly torched my apartment with my menorah last night?" Phil asked through the butt of a cigarette as he set his tool bag down.

"Why… does that… not… surprise me… in the slightest? I've known you… all of three days. You're the most… accident-prone… human being… I've ever seen." Beth chuckled, heart raging in her chest so hard she could feel the beats in her throat. "I mean… you defy Darwinism."

Her chuckle turned into a full-on belly-laugh.

After a tense silence, Phil lit the end of his cigarette and took a languid drag. "Why's this so funny to you? I nearly burned my building down on fucking *Hanukkah*."

"It's just," she snickered, "you shouldn't even be *alive* with as clumsy as you are. Especially with a job like this where you're working around heavy machinery and heights. With all due respect, you gotta work on your coordination."

"Thanks for that sage advice," he mumbled, "*kibitzer*."

A look of hurt and embarrassment flashed over Phil's leathery features. His kind eyes fell to the floor, and he wrapped his arms around his chest as if to hug himself. He pulled the tobacco-filled roll from between his lips, wiped the sweat and dirt from his forehead, and exhaled up at the textured ceiling.

Beth felt momentary regret at the comment despite the honesty behind it.

Seeing Phil genuinely hurt made her wish she hadn't opened her mouth. Staring at him silently, she truly soaked him in for the first time since they'd met. For someone his age, he was still fit with the frame of someone active and capable of the career path they'd both chosen.

And his face held a certain… *charm.*

Phil put the cigarette back between his chapped lips and held a hand in front of the door jamb, feeling heat seep outward through the crack.

"Oh boy." He frowned, pressed the lever, shoved his shoulder into the door, and launched into the machine room.

"Holy crap, it's sweltering in there!" Beth's eyes were large as she peered in from the landing. "I can feel it from all the way out here."

"Yup. That's no bueno," Phil grumbled through the filter in his mouth.

Beth set her tools down just inside the door and looked around. "I can't tell if I'm having a hot flash, dying from all those damn stairs, or if it is *actually* hot as hell in here."

"It ain't a hot flash, hun. This place is boilin'." He stole a glance at Beth's curvaceous frame and nervously ran a hand through his more-salt-than-pepper hair. "I can almost *guarantee* you that's why the elevator stopped. This room is supposed to stay below eighty degrees at all times."

"It feels like the fuckin' Arizona desert in here. How is that *possible?* It's literally *snowing* outside?"

"There's a ton of heat gain from the motors and this control box." He pointed to the large gray sheet-metal cabinet in front of them, roughly seven-feet-tall and another five feet wide.

Phil opened the thin, ventilated cabinet door of the controller box, exposing neat masses of circuitry, LEDs, wires, and soldered boards.

He stepped back at the waft of heat coming out of the door at him. "I was gonna tell you to double check the battery backup, but I don't think it's an issue of stuff not getting power, 'specially since all the other lights in the stairwell seem to be on."

"What do you think it *is* then?"

"Well, in a traction elevator like this," he motioned to the equipment in the cabinet, "these boards are designed to shut down on triggered relays in the event of a thermal overload so that the unit can't overheat and melt the thousands-of-bucks-worth of the computer-y shit inside."

Beth was silent, studying Phil with her eyes now.

"You see, Beth, inside, there's this bimetallic strip that, when it heats up, breaks the power supply and stops the current from hittin' the contractor coil. Deactivates the whole thing. Shuts it right down so the fucker doesn't fry."

Beth's eyes widened at the knowledge spewing from his mouth.

Moments ago, she'd thought he was just a bumbling klutz. Now, he was pouring out this wealth of knowledge.

She hated to admit it, but it was a little bit… sexy.

He looked around and put his hands on his hips. Tendrils of smoke oozed out of the cherry of the cigarette, one held dangerously-close to the loose strings hanging limply from his frayed belt.

"This room should have good ventilation and strong air conditioning to prevent this all from overriding and shutting down. The cooler you keep it, the easier everything is on the computer."

Beth nodded, watching diligently, catching a heavenly whiff of Phil's spiced aftershave.

"Who do we call to crank up the A.C.?"

"Well, I hear the A.C. runnin'." He pointed at the roof. "Hear it?"

She nodded.

"So that tells me somethin' could be blocking the ducts."

"Gotcha."

"We'll take a look through all of this gak first just to make sure nothin' got melted." He pointed to the cabinet full of circuitry again. "Then, we can divide and conquer and check the vents. If that's all it is, we can let it cool down and get the guy in the lift out with the drop key."

"You're pretty knowledgeable about this stuff," Beth said, offering the compliment genuinely.

"*Imagine that.*" He scoffed. "A job so simple, even a Darwin-defying dum-dum like *me* can do it."

"I didn't mean it like that. I just meant…" She shook her head and sighed, closing her mouth before she said something to make things worse.

"Alright, Beth, go in the kit and grab me the 11/32-inch socket and the Phillip's head, please," Phil said, no trace of pluckiness left in his voice. He reached up to study the small, red initial turnover tag made of metal that was pinned to the top of the machine.

Beth grabbed the socket, walked it over to him, placed the heels of each palm beneath his ears, and tugged gently upward.

He craned his neck and stared at her, jostled and confused. "Can I… *help* you?"

"You said grab the *Phillip's head.*" She smiled, soft and silly. "Get it? Phillip's… head?"

He just glared at her, features hard, lips pursed.

She pulled her hands away. "Because…
you're *Phil.*"

"I *know my name.*" His soft voice had an
edge of curtness to it.

With an awkward silence hanging
between them, she handed him the requested
tool and her smile fell.

"*Screwdriver. Please.*" He held out a
hand.

She retrieved it quickly and handed the
screwdriver to him. He used the end of it to
point at the metal tag dangling from the top
vents of the machine.

"It looks like the five-year service has
been completed, but the one-year service is
overdue. No one signed off on it." He
grimaced. "Boss's gonna be miffed about
that."

Beth hummed a confirmation despite not
having met their employer beyond her final
hiring interview a few days prior.

Phil pointed to two boxes full of levers
on his left. "Can you go check the cycles and
disconnects?"

"Sure." She nodded dutifully and started
to walk off, pausing by him for a moment.

"Sorry about what I said earlier. That wasn't nice. And, for the record, I'm glad you didn't burn your building down."

He forced a faint smile. "Thank you." He tossed his butt on the floor and snuffed it with his ratty work boot. Picking up the remnants, he stuck it in his back pocket to chuck in a bin later.

"Lit up the T.V. tray that it was on, too. By the time I found the fire extinguisher, the thing was black as asphalt. Melted my chocolate coins. Torched my dreidel. I'd had that thing for *years*. Now, there's soot all over the menorah. Whole thing's a friggin' mess."

"Well," she smiled, "tonight you wanna come over? We can light mine together if you want."

He perked up, fighting the shit-eating grin slowly forming beneath his gray beard. His heart fluttered, and he felt a zing of excitement rush through him like a shockwave.

"Yeah?"

"Sure. Why not? It's *mamosh* not a big deal." She shrugged, playing coy. "I mean, I was just going to have another quiet night in.

I was planning to stuff my face with *nosh* after I call and check in on my *bubbe*. I was gonna maybe have some cheese and make *latkes* and watch a movie or something."

"What movie?"

She shrugged, scanned the concrete machine room for a moment, and let her eyes settle back on the disconnects. "*Life Stinks*, maybe?"

"Classic. *The* most underrated Mel Brooks movie of all time. It's a travesty how few people have heard of that one."

"Agreed. I also really love *History of the World Part I*."

"Oh my God, don't even get me started. I used to have 'The Inquisition' song as my ringtone." He rubbed his neck. "I'd ask you to call me to prove it but I leaned too far over the railing and dropped my phone in the Hudson on my walk this morning."

"Whaaaaat? *You?* Totally out of character." Beth grinned.

"But yeah, if you're serious, I'll take you up on hanging out tonight. I can even bring donuts."

"Oh my God, we gotta stop talking about food right now. I'm friggin' starving."

"I know! I'm sorry!" He shuffled through his tool bag for a flashlight. "Enough kvetching. I promised you lox, and by God, it's comin' soon!"

They giggled almost in unison.

"Sounds like a plan."

"Good." Phil smirked.

Beth whipped her head around. "Wait, you gotta promise you won't burn my place down, okay? My apartment's rent-controlled, and I *really* like it there."

"I'll wear a bubble wrap vest and not touch a thing, I swear." He laughed. "I'll barely breathe."

Beth examined the boxes, scanning everything with unblinking eyes. "Everything looks fine over here far as I can see."

"Battery rescue's workin' fine. I can check the hoistway guide rails for debris later and inspect the sheave and cables after we get that *schmuck* outta there, but I think it's the heat that tripped it. So, if we can cool down the place, I can clear the faults and trips, check the L1 through L3 terminals, and do a manual reset. If that doesn't work, I'll have you inspect the flyweights inside the overspeed governor and all that good stuff."

"Sounds like a plan." She swiped her hands across her dark jeans. "So what do we do now?"

"Let's check for ventilation blockages." Phil pointed to one of the vents behind her.

She flashed a smile. "Aye-aye, Cap'n."

He tossed her the screwdriver. "Here. In case you need to take any stubborn grates off."

She shook it in the air and bee-lined for one of the vents.

Phil sought out the next one, holding a hand over the grate. "This one's blowing cold."

"This one, too." Beth hollered, leap-frogging toward the next one.

"This one's alright as well." He yelled at the next one.

Beth scuttled to the last one and held a hand up. "*Oy.* Major blockage in this one."

"Yeah?" Phil made his way over to her as Beth was nearly done unscrewing the vent's last screw.

"Yeah, looks like there's something soft stuffed up against it. Like the insides of a pillow or somethi—"

Beth didn't get the last of the word out before the grate swung open and the soft mound of cotton-like mush lurched like a fluffy, heaving mass. The second Beth's hands left the grate, a mischief of black rats shot out like bomb shrapnel, leaping onto her and Phil with violent force.

Beth screamed and fell backward onto the floor, shrieking as rats used her body as a landing pad.

Before Phil could even think about what he was doing, he hunched down, picking up fat rodents from atop Beth's chest and hurling them away with a windmill-type action, screaming all the while.

"*Mishegoss!*" he screamed at the top of his lungs as the last of the critters scurried off. He kicked at one, missing it, spinning his body wildly and nearly falling. He caught himself against a concrete wall just in the nick of time.

Beth shook and screamed, disgusted by the bombardment of the filthy creatures all-too-common in New York.

"What the *fuck* was that?!"

"I don't know!" He extended a hand to lift her up. "You okay? You hurt? Did you hit your head or anything?"

"No, I'm fine." She took his hand.

He pulled, losing his balance and nearly toppling back onto her. She rose, laughing at his consistent lack of coordination.

She chuckled nervously, "You're a real *mensch.* Thanks for tha—"

Just as the last syllable left her mouth, it was replaced by his lips.

Adrenaline and excitement coursed through her, first from the rodent attack and now from the gentle display of romantic affection. Her hands splayed up like a submissive hostage, but she didn't move away.

Something in her felt alive for the first time in a long time, fluttering giddily in her belly, warming her face despite the blast of ice-cold air pummeling them from the now-unobstructed vent.

She leaned in and relaxed her hands onto his shoulders and up through his hair as she kissed him back.

He pulled away, face blushing red across his smiling cheeks.

"That was… *wildly* inappropriate. I'm sorry."

She pulled her hands away from him, straightened her hair, and composed herself, feeling blush spread across her cheeks.

"*Don't be,*" she said, her voice barely a whisper.

Chapter 12

Twila's glossy eyes glittered with the shine of the overhead lights. She made a puckered face at the spiced, full-body taste of the whiskey that seemed to burn less and less with every sip.

"What's it like working with your Dad?" Twila asked, handing back the flask to Nathan.

He was propped on his elbows, legs stretched out beside hers. He snorted and took another long pull from the flask. "It's… fine, I guess."

"You know what fine stands for, right?"

His eyebrows rose. "No, what does it stand for?"

"Fucked-up, Insecure, Neurotic, and Emotional." She grinned. "F.I.N.E."

"Alright, well, it's *great* then," he said unconvincingly.

"You know what *great* stands for?" she asked with a smile.

"Oh, God, no. Do I even wanna know?"

"Doesn't stand for anything," she teased. "That was a test. You passed."

He shook his head. "You're ridiculous."

"I'm a *delight*."

Nathan peered at her through squinted eyes, body relaxed from the alcohol bounding through his system.

"He's a workaholic. He wasn't around a lot when I was growing up. I figured this would be a way to get to know him and have a little face-to-face time with him."

Twila's expression turned serious as she took the flask from him. He was taken aback by how beautiful she could be, even without her heart-stopping smile. As she fidgeted with the flask, his gaze wandered from her cerulean eyes to her luscious, pink lips.

He unconsciously licked his own, like a hungry lion stalking his prey through the tall grass of the Savannah.

She's probably wearing flavored lipgloss. Cherry, I'll bet.

He was overwhelmed with the urge to taste her.

"Are you getting the time with him that you wanted?"

Her question jolted him back to reality.

"No." He cleared his throat and straightened his back. "No, he's the same as he always was. Mercurial. Hard to read. Impossible to know."

She frowned. "That's… sad."

He chuckled softly, masking the pain. "Do I *look* sad? I'm cryin' all the way to the bank. You know as well as I do this company's never been more profitable. And thanks to me taking the reigns, we're branching out to all new territories. I may not have had the chance to do that if it wasn't for him being so hard to pin down."

She peered down at the atrium tree, dwarfed by their ridiculous height. "I worked with my Mom for a summer at her vet clinic. I couldn't do it. She was too controlling. Everything I did was wrong."

"Yup. Sounds familiar," he said with a nod.

"Yeah?" Twila's eyes shifted back to him.

"It wouldn't matter if I single-handedly landed a billion-dollar deal. It would never be good enough." Nathan blamed the whiskey coursing through his system for the overly truthful admission.

Twila crawled over and sat beside him. She hesitantly placed her hand on his, giving it a few gentle pats. "You're great at your job. He could've done a lot worse for VP. He should be proud."

"Thanks, but I don't need a pep talk." He sneered. "Let's just… drop it."

Twila sighed and put some distance between them. "Ugh. Nasty Nate strikes again."

His eyes darted toward hers. "*Nasty Nate?*"

"Before you started shitting on people around here, you used to be a really nice guy. I know you were the one who brought Margret the card when her dog died. When Tony tore that ligament in his knee, you did stuff for him for weeks until he was off the crutches. You anonymously sent flowers to Danielle after her divorce. I filed the receipt. We all used to like you. Now, you are just as miserable as—"

Holy fuck! Just shut up, Twila!

Nathan turned away.

She watched as Nathan's shoulders shook. Her scowl morphed into an expression of regret. The realization dawned on her that she'd made him… cry?

What have I done?

She rested her manicured hand on his shoulder. "Nathan, I—"

Suddenly, he erupted with laughter. Twila reeled back with a look of terror.

What is he, Dr. Jekyll and Mr. Hyde?

"Wow," he blurted out. "I *almost* care. Not quite, but *almost*."

Twila clenched her jaw until it ached. "You're… deranged."

Nathan's cackle rose from the depths of his toned stomach. "What? Has *Nasty Nate* hurt your *feewings?*" He faked a pout.

"You're a *prick*," she snapped.

"Maybe, but, unlike you, *I'm* still employed."

"Who is responsible for this?" Meredith asked, holding up a leather flogger in one hand and a shredded wad of wrapping paper in the other.

Caleb sheepishly held up his hand.

"Why?" Meredith's serious inquiry rose over the giggles and snickers of the other employees gathered around the present table.

"I saw you reading *Fifty Shades of Grey* on your lunch break a while back, and I just figured…" His bashful voice trailed off.

"So you thought, 'Let me get her a cat-o-nine-tails?'"

"It's a *flogger*, actually," he corrected.

Daniel cleared his throat, unimpressed. "This is not *work-appropriate*, guys."

Meredith glared at the head of Human Resources. As if she'd had any say in the matter…

From across the circle, James winked at her and mouthed, "Save it for later."

She rolled her eyes and tossed the flogger back on the table.

Daniel cleared his throat again, anxious to get on with the proceedings. "Next. *Caleb, it's your turn.*" He handed the man a present wrapped in snowflake wrapping paper.

The present was oblong and phallic. Caleb giggled and held it in front of his groin like a dong. "I see someone got me a gag gift."

Leonard cupped his hands around his mouth and shouted, "Looks like it's big enough to make *anyone* gag."

A few of the workers chuckled as Caleb unwrapped the gift. Dan was not amused.

Caleb's smile morphed into a look of disgust.

It was a black rotten banana in a half-gallon Ziploc bag, barely holding its form inside the peel.

"What the hell?" Caleb's eyes shot to Leonard. "You think this is *funny?*"

"I didn't give that to you. Damn, man. Chill."

"What kind of sick—"

"I did it," Mason held his hand up, laughing his ass off.

Caleb shot daggers at him with his eyes. "What the hell, man? Lester got a *Keurig*, and she's been employed here for, like, three minutes. I've been here two-and-a-half years, and you give me rotten fuckin' *fruit?*"

"That's not your *present*, you tool. That's payback for stealing the Brooklyn Regional Medical account from me, you *putz*."

"What the hell?! It was just the Rehab Center! It wasn't the whole account. They needed Bledsoe boots and ace bandages. I'm not gonna send them to Wound Care for that."

"Dude, I'm *messing with you!*" Mason half-growled-half-laughed, "Jesus, y'all *all* need to learn how to take a joke."

"I *hate* bananas."

"I know, *schmuck*. That's why I did it."

Mason reached around in the back pocket of his jeans and whizzed a smaller wrapped present through the air. Caleb flung the rotten banana onto the table beside him in a flash and caught the smaller package.

"Feliz Navidad, Cay-Cay." Mason grinned.

Caleb shredded the package like a pissed-off badger, face alight with childlike wonder as he figured out what it was. He held up another Ziploc, this one half the size, filled a third of the way with dried green marijuana flower.

"Merry Christmas, bud." Mason chuckled. "Get it? It's Christmas b—"

"Oh, I get it." Caleb rushed through the room and hugged Mason tightly. "*This* is why you're the best friend and roommate a dude can have."

"I know," Mason joked. "It's good shit, too. My uncle grows it on his farm in Kent. It's damn-near medical grade."

Daniel just stood, mouth slung open in shock. "You guys realize this is a work function, right?"

Caleb smiled at him. "Yeah, I'll wait til after to blaze up. Don't worry."

Daniel shook his head and handed a huge, odd-shaped present to Becca. "The last present is for you."

"Hmmmm, I wonder who this could be from." Her eyes stared straight at Laura, the only person who had not yet fessed up to one of the presents.

Laura smiled. "Open the square thing first."

Becca looked at the monstrosity before her and realized there were, in fact, two presents connected by an awkward belt of scotch tape. She pried the square present off and unwrapped it.

"A cookbook!" She looked at the back. "Healthy keto recipes for weight loss." She looked back up and cooed. "Thank you!"

"You're welcome! I know you gotta be bored with the same old stuff all the time." She motioned to the rest, fighting a smile. "Open the other one now."

Becca scrunched her brows as she lifted the heavy cylindrical object, about a foot and a half tall and several inches in diameter. As she shredded the paper off, she doubled over

with laughter and held up a shiny red fire
extinguisher for all to see.

Laura smirked. "I've seen you cook.
You're gonna need that."

Chapter 14

"Man, this party is fucking lame, dude," Mason whined.

"I know. If Zach were here…" Caleb said, throwing his head back and ducking past the shiny plaque that read 'Vice President' on the oak door leading into Nathan's office.

Mason groaned. "If Zach were here, this party'd be *wild*. He'd probably have a beer pong game going with the damned eggnog."

Caleb giggled. "He'd be three sheets to the wind right now. He wouldn't know what planet he was on."

"Rumor around the water cooler is he may have knocked up Meredith."

"That day on the copier?!" Caleb pointed to the wall behind him, mouth gaping in shock.

"Hard to know. James said Zach told him they were bangin' for a month before that."

"You believe that?"

"I dunno. If *James* said *he* was, I'd be like, 'Nah.' But since it's Zach, yeah, I mean, I think it could be true."

Mason pulled out one of the desk drawers, examining the contents, shuffling through pens, Post-its, and various medical product samples.

"I can't believe Nate shit-canned him."

"I can. He was caught slipping an employee the salami on the clock. What did he *think* would happen?"

"Why didn't he fire Meredith, too?"

"Fuck if I know. Does seem a little unfair now that you say it like that."

"Man, screw *Nasty Nate*." Caleb huffed petulantly in protest.

Mason opened another drawer, and his eyes lit up. "Ooooooh! Merry Christmas to *us*."

Caleb sat tall, trying to get a peek over the desk at Mason's find.

Mason held up an orange-tinged bottle of *Glenfiddich* with only a quarter remaining.

"Hoooooly shit. *Gran Reserva.* This is twenty-one-year-old scotch, dude."

"Oh, hell yes." Caleb set his solo cup on the desk and used his fingers like a billiard stick to tap it forward. "'Tis the season. Fill 'er up."

"No way, dude, what if Nate catches us?"

"Didn't you hear? Shit, he's stuck in the elevator." Caleb chuckled like a cartoon chipmunk. "He's been stuck in there for like two hours, dude. We're fine."

"What if he notices it's gone? I don't wanna lose my job over some dumb crap like this. I'm savin' for a PS5, dude."

"Don't be a pussy!" Caleb leaned across the desk and snatched the bottle from Mason's hand. He unscrewed the cap and poured nearly all the remnants into his solo cup."

"Dude, you are gonna get *schwasted.* You drink all of that, you're gonna be sweater-less in an hour, runnin' around screaming '*I'm Pickle Rick!*' and burping in everyone's face."

"I can't help it that my drunken state is full-on *Rick and Morty* fanboy." He offered the last of the booze to Mason, cocking his eyebrow.

"If we finish that, Nate's really gonna know someone broke in and messed with his stuff."

"So what?!"

"So that's like a three-hundred-dollar bottle of single malt."

"Fine. Pussy. Here, I'll just replace what I took."

"What?"

Caleb poured the last of the booze into his cup and set it down. Then he stood and unzipped his pants, reaching into his underwear for his dick. "You might wanna turn around. I'm about to unleash the hog."

"The *hog?*" Mason laughed, calling Caleb's bluff. "My money's on you having a micro-penis, you dildo."

"Suit yourself." Caleb pulled his cock out.

"Jesus, what the hell, man?!" Mason shielded his eyes.

"Don't be a little bitch about it. You were warned."

Caleb carefully positioned the bottle against the head of his dick and started urinating.

"First of all, wow, that *is* a freakin' *hog*." He gawked with envy for a moment. "Damn, I thought you were kiddin'."

"I don't kid about such serious matters, Mase." Caleb shook his head side-to-side slowly so as not to throw off the precarious positioning. He didn't want to accidentally urinate outside the bottle.

"Second, that is nefarious as hell. What if he *drinks* that?"

"Wish a motherfucker *would!* This one's for our homeboy, Zachary."

As Caleb's urination slowed to a dribble, he smiled. He tucked himself back into his pants, zipped, and set the bottle on the desk.

"Jesus, how dehydrated are you that your whizz is the same color as single-malt?"

Caleb just smiled proudly and rolled the warm bottle over toward Mason.

"You need to drink more water, man." Mason gagged dramatically, staring at the foamy liquid inside the bottle.

Caleb held up his loaded solo cup and winked. "That'll teach Nasty Nate to be such a fuckin' Grinch."

Chapter 15

Despite her valiant struggle, tears rolled down Twila's cheeks. She had turned her back to Nathan, standing in front of the cement wall, saying a silent prayer the doors would open soon. She couldn't stand another minute trapped in such close proximity with him.

She'd been fired.

Not that she was surprised after talking to her superior like she had.

People had been let go from Parramore Medical Supplies for a hell of a lot *less*. But the worst part wasn't that she was out of a job. It was that she was still stuck in a jammed metal box with him.

"Where the fuck are the maintenance people?" Twila snapped, wringing her hands together. "We've been here forever."

Nathan looked at his phone and then set it back down. "It's only been an hour and a half. Don't be dramatic."

"*Merry friggin'Christmas,*" Twila growled and cracked the heel of her foot into the metal wall. "We pay good money to keep this from happening."

"They're working on it. Calm down. We just have to wait it out."

Twila's eyes refocused on Nathan's. "I don't mind waiting it out. It's waiting it out with *you*. That's the problem. You just *fired* me. Next, you'll tell me I'm too sensitive, or say that Sir Puffington's too fat, or that I'm *breathing* too loud…"

They each took to a side of the elevator and sat, staring down at their laps, grasping their phones in desperate attempts at distraction. After a few moments of silence, Nathan's hands dropped to his sides, along with his phone.

"Sir… *Puffington?*"

She shook her head. "*Seriously?*"

"What?"

"It's my cat's name. I've brought him here *several* times!" She was offended.

"Everyone knows who that is, except for *you*, apparently."

She whipped out her phone and scrolled through her camera roll, unwilling to make eye contact with him.

Feeling contrite, he snorted. "That's a… *creative* name for a cat."

"He's got a *glandular* disorder. That a problem?"

"Not at all. I would never fat shame your cat. Or *any* cat." Nathan was unable to keep a smile from creeping on his face. "Sir Puffington. So he was knighted and everything? You must be so proud."

"I am actually. I'm sure you wouldn't know that. You probably have never had pets."

"On the contrary, I have a Jack Russell *terror* waiting at home right now."

Twila laughed at the play on words.

"Her name is Lulu. She's probably whizzed all over the place. She's getting incontinent in her old age."

Twila's disposition softened. "So there *is* a heart in there somewhere. Hmm. You hide it well."

He shrugged, feeling a bead of sweat roll down the back of his neck. The elevator was slowly turning into a sauna, and he was out of layers appropriate to shed.

"So, is your boyfriend with Mister Puffington tonight?" He cursed himself silently for inquiring. Nathan wanted to act dispassionate, but genuine curiosity gnawed at him.

Twila knew what he was getting at but still answered. "It's *Sir* Puffington, and I don't have a boyfriend. Why?" She narrowed her eyes at him.

"Just makin' polite conversation." He looked down at the floor. "I considered bringin' her in but didn't want to have to wrangle her all night. She's probably sitting on the couch watching *Portlandia* right now."

Twila chuckled.

A comfortable silence settled over them for the first time since the debacle had begun.

"Hey." She looked back at him, chewing her lower lip.

His eyes found her, unable to tear his gaze from her glossy lips. He suddenly wished they were on his own…

"Wanna see a picture of my puss?"

Nathan's blood turned to ice at the question. The answer was a resounding 'Yes,' but the boldness of the inquiry confused him. "Um... I'm sorry. Did I just *hear* you right?"

"My *cat*." Twila winked. "Get your mind outta the gutter, perv." She scooted to his side, close enough that their arms were touching.

The contact made her buzz with nervous energy. She fought to ignore it and held up the gallery on her phone. On the screen was a morbidly obese black and brown Manx with a mustache of white hair amid the feline's predominately dark face.

Nathan laughed. "The name is ridiculous, but it's actually sorta fitting. With the fluffy body and the full, regal look about him. Yeah," he nodded, "I can see it now."

"Right?!" She smirked. "I showed you mine. Now, you show me yours."

He froze at the comment and then quickly realized she was requesting a photo of Lulu. The heat in the elevator was starting to derail his train of thought.

"I gotta see the kind of poor pup who has to put up with you."

"Lulu doesn't put up with me. She *loves* me."

"Dogs love everyone," she teased.

He pushed the power button to wake his phone and held it up. "She's my background."

"Aww!" Twila softened as she examined the photo plastered on his lock-screen.

"Wanna see more?"

"Sure!" Twila cleared her throat, trying to reel her excitement back in.

Nate flipped through the pictures on his cell until more images of the Jack Russel terrier appeared on the screen. He paused on one. A mostly-white canine with a black mask in a purple knitted sweater stared back, snug beneath a lifted comforter. "She gets cold. She likes to wear sweaters."

But Twila almost didn't realize there was a dog in the photo. Beside the canine was a man, from his hardened pecs down to his muscular thighs, clad in nothing but turquoise boxer briefs that boasted a large package tucked within.

It was Nathan.

The searing visual of his body made Twila want to salivate as though she'd just smelled a sizzling ribeye steak. A wave of heat raced up Twila's neck, bathing her face in a pink hue. She couldn't shake the arousing image of his abs and the bulge in his briefs.

Finally, Twila smiled. "Gorgeous."

Oblivious, Nate turned off the display and set the device on the floor. "Yeah, she's somethin'. She's like a wind-up toy most of the time. She's especially cute when she's asleep."

They sat beside one another for a moment, each taking a turn at stealing a glance at the other.

Finally, Nathan spoke. "You're not fired. I… lashed out. You're good at what you do. Dad and I have been impressed on several occasions by some of your proposals in the quarterly budget meetings. Everyone is so stuffy and monotone, but you present like your heart is clearly in this. Almost like you see something exciting in the numbers that nobody else can see."

"Whatever I do, I put my whole ass into it."

He laughed and shook his head at the ridiculous comment.

"Thank you for not firing me." She looked into his eyes long and hard. "I am sorry for how I spoke to you."

He waved it off. "Under the bridge."

After a beat, she groaned. "Aww, man, we're supposed to be up there," she pointed to the top corner of the elevator, "getting sloppy drunk with the people we already spend too much of our lives around."

Nathan had a hearty laugh and nudged her with his shoulder, "And here you are, stuck with your dickhead boss in a cramped elevator."

"The struggle is real."

They laughed. A moment later, their eyes caught one another. Nathan grinned and swept back a blonde curl behind her ear with a gentle finger.

"Tell me you didn't just do the thing where the guy sweeps the girl's hair behind her ear." Instead of chuckling, she glanced down at his mouth, feeling breathless.

His warm brown eyes bore into hers. Tensed muscles flexed as he adjusted himself, blood vacating from his brain and flowing south. He could see the desire on her face. He could *feel* it in her body language.

He felt it, too, the lust for her making his cock ache with a mixture of pleasure and pain. Excitement surged through him as the frustration from their entrapment melted into aching want.

Goosebumps rose on her flesh as millions of tiny hairs reached for what her body desperately craved.

Him.

"Why are you looking at me like that?" she whispered, leaning into him a millimeter at a time as if pulled by some unseen force.

"Like *what?*" he mumbled, staring at her stunning lips.

Her voice was laced with a quiet, wanton intensity. "Like a wolf who wants to eat me for dinner."

"I can't help it." He flashed a sensual smile and leaned closer. "I see something I want to devour." He felt her shiver and leaned closer.

Twila held his smoldering gaze, unsure if she had ever been so turned on.

This was Nathan Dupont, the headlining lead actor of two years' worth of nighttime vibrator fantasies…

Ever since that night, he shoved her against the copier and allowed his skillful tongue to take the reins.

Beyond the elevator, they could hear laughter and music, but inside, they were in their own little world.

Disconnected.

Intimate.

Nathan placed a curled finger beneath her chin and drew her to a spot mere inches from his lips.

"As much as I want you right now," his eyes swept the whole length of her, soaking her in, "and I do, I won't do anything unless you want me to."

The silence between them was thick, and Twila felt the painful throb of desire between her thighs.

"*If you want this,*" Nathan swiped his thumb over her bottom lip, "*just say yes.*"

Never blinking, Twila uttered a breathless "*Yes.*"

Nathan claimed her lips with his own, kissing her with a hunger, a raging desire he didn't know himself capable of. His hand shifted to her neck and hair, eagerly pulling her closer as their interaction reached a fever pitch.

She pulled him toward her trembling body by the t-shirt, tongue whirling against his. Her nipples hardened, protruding through her thin lace bra. Fire erupted in her belly as her body vibrated with excitement and a burst of insatiable lust.

A flash of white-hot heat rushed between his legs as Nathan's cock stiffened. It struggled against the confines of his pants, engorged and throbbing, fueled by her sugar-sweet lip gloss. All logic escaped his mind as her fingers slid into his hair, pulling him tightly to her.

She straddled him against the wall. Their bodies feverishly melded with one another in a singular, undulating beast, all grasping hands and delicious tongues.

Nathan's warm hands made their way to her breasts, massaging them reverently through her sweater. She gasped against his mouth at the rush of adrenaline. His touch made her body writhe, surging with the need to feel him inside of her.

He kissed her again. Slower. *Deeper.*

Twila pulled away just enough to speak, the skin around her mouth red and agitated. "Nate," she panted.

His name on her sweet, pouty lips made him even harder. He nudged her curls aside with his nose and whispered, "*Yes?*"

"We shouldn't do this." Her eyes fluttered closed at the feel of his hands sliding beneath her sweater, caressing the bare skin beneath. "Nathan, we *work* together. You're my fucking *boss*."

"Look at me, Twila."

She did.

They held each other's eyes for what felt like an eternity. The atmosphere was electrified, as if lightning had struck the elevator, incinerating all of the common sense and logic within, leaving only desire and sexual tension in its wake. His thumbs grazed her nipples through her bra, and she slid her hands through his thick hair. They were two magnets, ones hell-bent on touching.

"We can stop… if that's what you want. We can be good and, you know, pretend this never happened."

The words made his hard-on throb painfully in an act of pure rebellion.

Twila's heart thudded in her chest. "No. Not this time. Not again."

She laid a soft, sensual kiss on the taut skin of his neck, feeling his jugular pound beneath a thin layer of close-shorn stubble. Her trail of kisses led up, stopping at his ear. She nuzzled it with her nose and whispered, "This time, *I don't wanna be good.*"

Chapter 16

Twila's fingers tore at the bottom of Nathan's t-shirt, yanking it overhead and discarding it in the corner. His hands worked to pull off her sweater, getting it stuck on her chin and nose. She giggled, giddy, and resumed kissing him once it had been shed.

Nathan stared at her bra bursting with milky cleavage, wanting to devour every inch. Her perky nipples poked through the gaps in the lacy fabric, begging for contact from his hot tongue. He obliged, tracing his tongue around each before sucking them gently through the lace. Twila arched her back and moaned.

"*Shhh.*" Nathan chuckled, whispering his request to quiet herself. "If we could hear Becca, if anyone has an ear to the door, they'll be able to hear us. I promise, next time, you can be as loud as you want." He grinned and trailed a fingertip down her collarbones to one of her breasts. "In fact, I encourage it highly."

"Mmmmm. *Next time?*" She offered a sly grin. "That's a bit presumptuous. What if you're a terrible lay?"

"Ohhhh, babydoll, I assure you I'm not. I don't just work hard in business. I am not afraid to work those long hours to make sure I get the job done right."

The implications of his comment and the sudden appearance of the sexy little pet name sent a surge of warmth down between her legs. She could feel her panties growing wetter by the second. *"Good answer."*

A knee-weakening grin crept across Nathan's jaw. "I want to make you come until you *beg me to stop.*"

The words coming from his lips made Twila want to faint. She needed this. After years of longing glances and thoughts about the kiss they shared, this was long-awaited.

He grabbed her firm ass and pulled her tight to him, pressing her against his erection.

Twila unbuttoned his slacks, inching the zipper down. With nimble hands, she pushed her fingers beneath the fabric of his pants and boxers to the throbbing cock below. Nathan stifled a moan and stared up at Twila like she'd awakened an animalistic part of him that wanted to rip her clothes off with his teeth. He savored the feel of her supple skin beneath his palms and the taste of his favorite whiskey on her tongue. She glistened with dewy perspiration, skin scorching beneath his tender touch.

He brushed the backs of his fingers against her cheek, an act both sweet and intimate. *Loving*.

Twila moved his index finger to her lips, taking it deep into her mouth, twirling her tongue as she slipped it in down to the base.

A small taste of things to come.

Nathan felt like all of the air had been sucked out of the room. He soon replaced the finger with his tongue, slipping it against her own with passion.

He rose to his knees, taking her in the air with him, and lowered her onto her back on the cold, marbled chevrons that adorned the floor. He pressed against her, his pelvis grinding between her spread legs. She squirmed beneath him, furiously yanking down the waistband of her forest green leggings.

"How do I…?" He struggled with the stretchy apparel. Nathan wanted to shred them right off her.

She smiled against his lips. "Here. Let me. These are a pain." She shifted out from beneath him, rose to her feet, stripped the bottoms off, and kicked them aside.

Nathan stared at her like she was a statue of Venus, a goddess in her own right.

"You are a fucking vision," he said, following the curves of her long legs up to her lacy, white thong. He wanted her thighs wrapped around his ears.

Her body beckoned for his touch like a siren's call. Nathan was where he felt he belonged… on his knees before the gorgeous deity, about to unburden his most lust-soaked sins. His erection strained against the opening of its briefs, aching to be freed.

With both hands, he pulled her thong down, allowing the soaked panties to drop silently to the floor.

He pressed his face to her mound, burying his face between her thighs, licking her clit with languid, calculated strokes. He coaxed her toward him with the flick of his skilled tongue.

Her head lolled backward. She braced herself, pressing her hands against the brass wall above him. Nathan's hand moved between her legs, skimming the tender flesh as his fingers traced their way up to her pussy. He parted her skin with his fingers and glided them through her wetness. Inch by agonizing inch, he eased one inside of her, feeling her warmth tighten around him. As she stifled a moan, the finger retreated, only to be replaced by two. He coaxed with gentle digits, sucking her delicate clit all the while.

She felt the warmth between her legs spread as he worked his talented fingers and eager mouth on her intimate spots, edging her ever closer to an orgasm.

"Fuck, you taste as amazing as you look," he mumbled into the thin, manicured

strip of honey-blonde hair between her legs. *"I can't get enough of you,"* he mumbled again before slipping his tongue deep inside her, feeling her pulsing vagina constrict and relax against him with every unrelenting plunge.

Her body shuddered as the words finally registered in her ear.

As he slipped his fingers inside her again, it was just enough to send her over the edge. A rippling orgasm rocked her to the core. She clenched her teeth and trembled, trying in vain to stifle the growl within her. Her legs shook, clenched feet juddering with adrenaline and excitement from the stimulation.

Satisfied, Nathan's brown eyes stared up, watching her squirming with each gripping wave of the aftershocks. He rose to his feet and pressed his mouth to hers, allowing her to taste herself on his tongue.

Her hands tore at his pants, unbuttoning them and pushing them down to the floor, followed quickly by his black boxer briefs. His erect cock sprung, and she melted at the feel of its thickness in her hand.

"Hold on a second," he panted, reaching down into his pants and fishing out his wallet. He pulled a foil square from it and set the condom within free with his anxious digits.

She took it from him without a word and lowered to her knees. Before placing it on, she took his cock into her mouth, savoring the sweet taste of his pre-cum on her slick tongue.

He ran his fingers through her hair and thrust gently, slowly, each time pressing a few millimeters closer to the back of her hot throat. She stared up at him, over his toned abdomen, with watery eyes. She looked so beautiful there, taking him to the hilt with enthusiasm.

Nathan pulled away, and Twila eagerly rolled the rubber on. He lowered himself to the floor and freed her breasts from her bra, drawing one of her nipples gently between his teeth. She shuddered again against him as he wrapped an arm around her waist and laid her down. He ran a finger along her glistening slit and smiled as she gasped again. The sound was music to his ears.

He scooped his arms behind her bent knees, parting her trembling legs forcefully before pressing himself in tight between them.

Twila panted, body aching for the sensation of his fullness, feeling the heat radiating from his veiny cock against her delicate, pale skin.

She arched her back, allowing him inside, sinking her fingers into his muscular shoulders as his cock sunk deep into her.

He clutched her flexed legs tight in the crooks of his arms and watched her face flash red, back arched like a peach horseshoe with the pleasurable sensation.

He pulled back all the way until he was barely inside of her pulsing opening. He waited for a moment, soaking in the look of desire in her blue eyes, hearing the breathy "fuck me" chanted from her lips. She was beautiful there.

Nathan bore down and plunged deep again. Fucking Twila felt like nothing he'd ever experienced before. The thought of this ending, the thought of them going their separate ways after this, felt like it would shatter his soul in fragments. She was pleasure in the purest form.

He wanted more of this. More of *her*.

And not just tonight, but every night to come.

Chapter 17

"Alright, the system's coolin' off now, but I'm gonna let it get down another ten degrees before I do the manual override. If this thing fries, boss'll have our ass," Phil said, wiping his palms on his ratty pants.

"Copy that," Beth said, glancing at the wad of shredded material the rats had been using to nest in the vent.

"You know how to use a drop key?"

"Yeah, I haven't personally, but I've watched it done. I saw the other guy, Lance, use one in Hell's Kitchen on Monday. Didn't look hard."

"It's cake. You've seen the back of a hoistway door, right? And the two knobs?"

"Yep, I understand the concept."

"Okay. Groovy. You know how to use a chock?"

"Same thing. Seen it, but never done it."

"Right on. Grab it out of that bag."

She followed orders, retrieving a tiny mechanism with a twist knob on top designed for safely holding elevator doors in their open position.

"Alright, so I'm gonna stay up here and check the motor and the sheave and inspect the over-speed governor and flyweights 'n shit. You take both drop keys and the chock down to thirty-two. See if you can get the guy stuck in it out before he takes a dump in one of the corners. That'll be a nightmare."

"Aye-aye, Cap'n." She saluted him and started making her way down the numerous flights.

Chapter 18

Nate flashed a half-smile at the look of pleasure on her face, taking in her dewy skin and curly mess of blonde hair that framed her panting face.

Twila savored the delicious friction that came with every achingly slow, deliberate thrust. She closed her eyes, relishing the ragged sound of his breath tangled with her own as he fucked her hard and deep. With *feeling*.

His pace increased, and Twila felt his orgasm build.

"Mmmm, God damn, Twila. You feel so good." A groan escaped him, pace quickening.

Twila couldn't speak. She could only moan, cheeks on fire, breath hitching as her nails dragged across his deltoids and back.

She tilted her hips, allowing Nathan to penetrate her deeper, filling her.

He kissed her hard and growled into the soft flesh of her throat, feeling her pulse pounding against his face. Finally, he whispered, *"Come for me again, babydoll."*

"Yeah?" she cooed, face crimson.

"Mmmm-hmmm. I want you to come with me."

Twila moaned into Nate's ear as her body relaxed. Her eyes closed, and her face contorted. *"Fuuuuuck,"* she purred.

Mere moments later, Twila felt herself tip over the abyss into a sea of pleasure yet again, riding pulsing waves of orgasmic bliss, savoring the fullness of his buried cock. Every muscle below her navel pulsed and throbbed as she came, dragging her teeth along his rock-hard shoulder to keep from screaming.

He cradled her to his chest lovingly, feeling her judder and quake against him. *"That's right."* He stroked her hair, pressing slowly into her again until another wave ripped through her.

Twila gasped, tensing like concrete beneath his chiseled form, seized in panic.

A stripe of light danced across the floor before them…

Like something ethereal and heavenly…

"N-Nathan," Twila finally mustered.

"*Oh dear, sweet God!*" A woman hollered.

Nathan whipped his head around, scrambling to find the source of the foreign voice that sounded all too real to be a figment of his imagination.

Twila recognized the voice immediately.

It was *Becca*.

Drunk and appalled.

Twila screamed from beneath Nate's naked body as their eyes connected with another woman, stocky and older with short, drab hair, one that neither Twila nor Nate had ever seen before.

The woman stood frozen in the open doorway of the elevator's cab. Beyond her were the stunned, familiar faces of Parramore employees, gawking.

"Jesus!" Nathan growled as he scrambled for something to cover up with.

The maintenance worker turned around to give them privacy, nervously tapping the drop key in her palm.

"Um, uh, *hi.*" Beth squatted, still keeping her back to them. She placed the chock in the hoistway door and tightened the screw. "I'm Beth. I'm here to extract you from this metal shoebox."

Audible gasps and giggles wafted in through the open doors.

Nathan grabbed the first thing in sight and threw it on, cupping his exposed privates in his hand. Twila hid behind him, naked, wishing she could curl up and die so she would never have to face her co-workers again.

"Um, can we have a moment, please?" Nate yelled.

"Sure, um, do you want me to take the chock out, or…"

"Yes! *For the love of God, close the door!*"

As Beth removed the safety device and started to squeeze the door closed, Nate stood in front of the gathering gaggle of employees. His handsome face had turned burgundy with embarrassment. With eyes cast down to the floor, he cleared his throat, wearing only Twila's ugly sweater, which read: *Jingle My Balls*.

Chapter 19

Three mortifying minutes later, Nathan and Twila breached the hoistway door, doing their walk of shame out into the office foyer where Lauren was crooning a drunken version of Aerosmith's *Love in an Elevator* into the karaoke machine's corded microphone.

Twila and Nathan adjusted their disheveled clothes and hair, both humiliated.

Twila leaned into his ear and whispered over the music, staring at the gawking co-workers. "I feel like I'm reenacting Cersei Lannister's walk of shame."

Nathan couldn't help but snicker at the thought of their co-workers chanting *"Shame!"* as they passed.

Nathan stepped onto the karaoke stage, arms folded, and waited for Lauren to finish.

Smug, she handed over the mic to him. "All yours, VP."

Nathan took the microphone and addressed the employees. Twila watched, mortified, with a hand covering the majority of her face.

"Excuse me, thank you all for your attention. I apologize for what you all just witnessed. That was unprofessional and, I'm sure, *scarring* for some of you."

"Heyyy," Caleb slurred. "Didn't you fire Zach for, like, the sssame thing?"

Nate looked down at the floor, face solemn. "Yes. I realize this makes me look like a hypocrite. I assure you it will never happen again." His eyes met Twila's, and he couldn't help but smile. He tried to fight it. "Well, *here*, at least."

Twila blushed again, this time at his words.

"I am going to leave you all here to celebrate. But first, there is the matter of the Ugly Sweater Party prize..."

"It better not be a bike," Laura hollered before subtly stepping behind Twila to shield herself from Nathan's view. Then, Laura looked around and mouthed, *'Who said that?'*

"Looking around, I want to commend you on all taking part in the festivities." He stared at the image of Keanu Reeves with the golden deity halo on Lester's shirt and snickered. "*Nice.*"

"Thanks." A smile crept onto Lester's tan, cherubic face.

"Is this everyone?" Nathan asked.

"No, Meredith is in the bathroom blowin' chunks," Becca said.

"Lucky *Chunks.*" Caleb snickered.

"No," Meredith's mousy voice said, "I'm here." She stepped forward. Nathan was appalled by her hideous sweater.

He looked around for a moment before his eyes settled on the drunken Caleb and his 8-bit style sweater of Santa riding a unicorn excreting a rainbow out of its ass. He plucked three envelopes from the parka pocket in his arms, layered beneath the swath of cashmere scarf. "This year, I decided to do three prizes instead of one."

"Is one of them a bike?" Laura asked, clearly annoyed at the entire concept.

"No," Nathan laughed. "None of these are bikes."

He held up one envelope. "Third place goes to Meredith because… whatever that is… should be burned." He motioned to her sweater with the envelope.

With a timid hesitation, she retrieved it from him and tore it open. Her eyes grew wide. "It's a… is this real?"

"Yes. Eight *hundred* dollars in gift cards."

"*Jesus Christ!*" Mason shouted from the far end of the employee lineup.

"Wow, thank you, sir!" Meredith ran up and wrapped Nathan in a hug.

He looked over her shoulder at Twila, who was beaming, face glowing from the recent sex. "You're welcome. Merry Christmas."

As Meredith stepped away, he spoke again. "Second place is you, Caleb."

Caleb hiccuped. His head shot over the group like a groundhog. "What?"

"I didn't know unicorns could diarrhea rainbows, but that monstrosity will haunt my dreams. Great Job." He offered an envelope with the words 'Second Place' on it.

Caleb stumbled forward and took it. "Wow."

"It's any five paid days off of your choosing next year to use in addition to your regular paid vacation and sick days. You know the drill. Just get with Holly so she can get them on the calendar."

Caleb was speechless. "I… gotta… go *do* something…" He pointed to the bank of offices behind them and bolted without another word, anxious to replace the piss-filled bottle in Nathan's desk with all the cash in his wallet. Hopefully, it would be enough.

"Okayyyyy." Nathan moved on to the first-place winner. "First place goes to newcomer Lester. I don't know where you found that damn sweater, but it's the ugliest, weirdest thing I've maybe ever seen. Well done."

He handed Lester the final envelope.

"It's a three-day all-expense-paid cruise in late January."

The gaggle of people gasped.

Mason smacked Laura with his shoulder and murmured, "Guess he's not such a frickin' Grinch after all."

Nathan smiled at the Parramore workers before him. "There's one more thing." He paused, long and thoughtful. "You all work very hard for this company. We would be unable to do what we do without *you*. My father and I have been discussing a way to thank you and to show you you're appreciated for a few weeks now. It's not much, but sales were phenomenal in Q3. You will all see our gratuity reflected in your future paychecks because we have decided to give a one-and-a-half-dollar raise across the board to show our appreciation."

The crowd stood in stunned silence.

Mason started a slow clap.

Everyone else followed suit except for Twila, who only stared at him with bright blue eyes and blushing cheeks.

Chapter 20

Half an hour later, Nathan and Twila made their way down the last floor of the lackluster stairwell. They funneled into the gleaming lobby, punctuated with all of its polished accents of metal and marbled stone.

"I'm so glad to be out." Twila breathed a deep, relieved sigh and glanced at the brass doors of the elevator.

Nathan couldn't help but smile as he watched her. She was stunning beneath the warm glow of the lobby's lights.

From the front desk, Jessie smiled at them. "Glad to see you're both okay! I was so worried when I heard you two got stuck in there."

Twila's shoulders relaxed, grateful the news of their vulgar indiscretion had not spread to the receptionist.

"We're fine, Jessie. Thank you." She turned to Nathan and leaned close. "I know eventually this will be funny, but right now, I feel *mortified.*"

"Same." Nathan snickered. "I guess I earned my nickname today."

As they reached the rotating front door, Twila's smile fell, weighed down by where to go from here. "I guess I should head home and get that Chinese order in. Christmas Story comes on at eight."

"You hungry?"

"Starving. I can't believe Mason forgot the dip. All I've had all day is bagel and…"

She blushed, suddenly remembering something she more *recently* had in her mouth.

Nathan tucked a stray strand of hair behind her ear and smirked. He used a crooked finger to tilt her chin up, lifting her eyes to his, nearing her face. "Let me buy you dinner tonight. I'll take you to *Exquise.*"

Her eyebrows raised. "That place costs a *fortune.*"

"So…" he grinned, "it's a date?"

Her cheeks grew rosy again as she fought the urge to smile. "So what we did… it wasn't… just like a *heat of the moment* thing?"

"God, no. I mean, wait… was it for *you?*"

Bashful, she shook her head.

"Okay, good." He moved a little closer. "I'd like to take you out. That's if Sir Puffington can fend for himself for a few more hours tonight."

"Oh, he's fine. He wouldn't even know I was gone. He's pretty aloof."

"So, dinner then?"

"Hmmm," Twila hummed bashfully, looking down at the patterned floor.

"For dessert, I will buy you the best hot cocoa around. There's a place nearby that puts these, like, homemade marshmallows in it. It's delicious."

"Yeah?"

"Yep," he pulled her into his embrace, warm and caring. "Then, if you're up for it, I'll take you for a walk after…"

"It's thirty *degrees* outside." Her eyes peered into his. "It's supposed to snow tonight."

"Yes, but there's a couple-block area near my place where all the trees are lit up right now for this big festival of Christmas lights. When it's snowing, it is fucking *magical*."

"Cocoa and Christmas lights? Who'd have ever thought Nasty Nate had so much holiday spirit?"

Nate kissed her, slow and soft, feeling an addictive rush at her very touch. When he finally pulled away, he said, "So… you'll go?"

She nodded.

"Good. It's a date." He planted a small kiss on her forehead and pulled away to wrap his neck in his scarf. "What about tomorrow? You busy?"

"No." She pulled her gloves on, beaming.

"Ever been ice skating down at Rockefeller Center?"

She whipped her head around and stomped her foot in a sudden, wild reaction.

"I've always wanted to do that! I was just saying that!"

Nathan laughed and scrubbed a mark on the floor with the sole of his shoe. "Yeah, me too. Too nervous to do it alone, though. I figure this way, if you're there, you can keep me from falling on my ass."

Twila beamed at him, marinating in the electrified silence between them.

"Deal. Sounds fun." She smiled and stared out into the dusky light beyond the spinning door, studying the frosty shadows of the looming skyscrapers outside.

"I'm going to run home and get cleaned up. I will see you at the restaurant in a bit? Say, eight o'clock?"

She nodded. "It'll be fun."

"I think so, too." He laughed. "Though, it certainly can't be the *worst* part of your day after being locked in an elevator all afternoon."

"That's a plus." She giggled. "Although, if I had the choice to do it all again, I would. You know... considering how it all worked out."

"Yeah, me too." He smiled. "Minus the witnesses there at the end."

She doubled over with laughter and covered her blushing face with her knitted gloves. "Yes!"

"Plus, that party looked lame." He shrugged. "I got the better deal here. Being trapped in a brass box with you beats an *Ugly Sweater Party* any day."

About Aurora

Aurora Alba is a writer of contemporary romance, paranormal romance, fantasy, and mystery.

She hails from a small town in Wyoming and writes with the full support of her husband and fur-babies. She strives to be a captivating storyteller.

Aurora has published books in other genres under her real name, Heather Wohl, and another pen name, H.M. Wohl.

Love, in all forms, is her passion.

About Odessa

Odessa is an award-winning filmmaker and a cancer survivor who spent over a decade working in the film industry. However, storytelling has always had a spell over her.

Born in Wyoming and spending most of her adult life in Florida and Louisiana, she now lives on the beach in New England with her boyfriend and their two pups. When she isn't writing, she's usually tending to her massive vegetable garden or kayak fishing.

Odessa Alba is a romance pen name (an easy way to keep her genre fiction separate for readers.) She has published several horror novels under her real name, Erica Summers, and also writes cozy mysteries under the pen name Trixie Fairdale.

A Note From The Ogres

Even though this book was proofread thoroughly by professionals, beta readers, and ARC readers… mistakes happen. We want our readers to have the best experience possible. If you spot any spelling, grammatical, or formatting errors, please feel free to reach out to us at:

Rustyogrepublishing@gmail.com

Reviews

If you could take the time to leave an honest review after you've read this book, we would greatly appreciate it. We respect your time and promise it doesn't *have* to be long and eloquent. Even a few words will do!

As a small publishing house, every review helps others determine if this book is right for them and greatly increases our chances of being discovered by someone else who might enjoy it.

The
Billionaire's
Assistant
Odessa Alba
A NEW ENGLAND BILLIONAIRES BOOK

The Billionaire's Assistant

Book one of the New England Billionaire's Series. Available worldwide in ebook, paperback, hardcover. Audiobook releasing in May of 2024.

Welcome to New England, home of scenic beaches, dazzling autumn foliage, and swoon-worthy affluent billionaires. Hindered by a broken arm, Eric Salko's life is upended when the VP of his investment firm, Rob, hires him a temporary new personal assistant. The moment the stunning employee enters his palatial Greenwich, Connecticut estate, all bets are off.

With her life in shambles, Kira Blumquist is desperate to make the most of her lucky break, but the growing attraction to her new boss threatens to jeopardize everything. Like a moth to a flame, she soon secretly finds herself yearning for his forbidden touch.

Odessa Alba's sensual series debut sizzles with smoldering heat, opulence, and a heartwarming HEA.

Call of the Wyld
OF
the
A DESTORIAN ADVENTURE NOVELLA
Heather Wohl

Call of the Wyl

*A Standalone Destorian Fantasy Novella with
a dash of paranormal romance*

Available worldwide in ebook and audiobook

**What would it take to send your own brother
to the dungeons?**

Wyl bounty hunter, Brutus, is in hot pursuit of
his elusive brother, Otis. With a bounty on his
sibling's head (and Brutus in desperate need
of fast coin) he must bring his own relative to
justice. Along his mysterious journey, Brutus
finds himself in the clutches of Brute Fest, a
violent festival where black eyes and vicious
brawls are celebrated. His trip takes an even
more intriguing turn when he becomes
enraptured by a rose-gold beauty named
Violet. Captivated by the wild, new world
around him, Brutus must make an impossible
choice between love, money... and family.

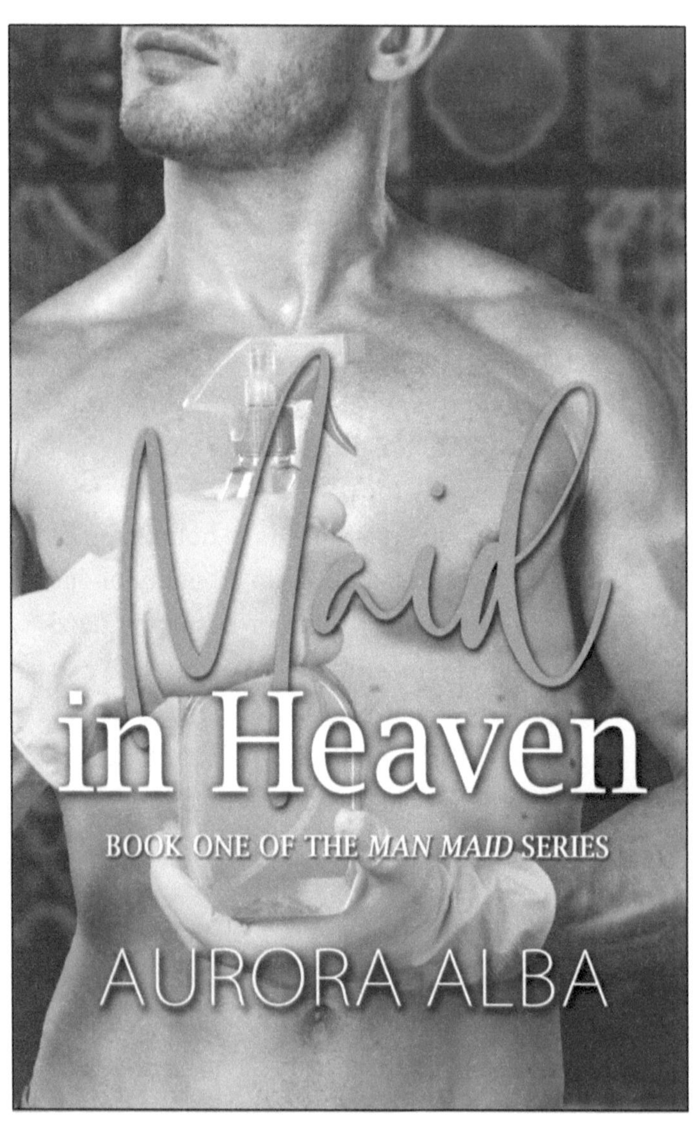

Maid
in Heaven
BOOK ONE OF THE MAN MAID SERIES
AURORA ALBA